The Maidens of Fey &
Other Dark Matter

By
Stacey Dighton

Cover Drawing: Jayden Dighton

Also by Stacey Dighton:

Pale Face & The Raven

DEDICATION

To mum and dad. Thanks for being the most supportive parents that a loud, long haired, stubbornly independent and slightly crazy kid could wish for. Love you loads.

CONTENTS:

The Maidens of Fey

Have you ever been on a trip to a new and strange place and from the very moment you arrive you realise that something is off? Something is....well, something is different. Perhaps you don't pick up on it at first or maybe you're just too tired to notice, but within a couple of hours, or even a day, you start to sense a resonance, a flicker or vibration if you will. Perhaps you've woken in the middle of the night in a cold sweat, or you've spent the whole day with a feeling of something heavy and foreboding hanging around your neck, you're feet seemingly trawling through thick and gloopy syrup. Perhaps you've decided that you simply don't like the place because it's....well it's different. Or because it drags you back to a foggy memory of your childhood that you're certain is not pleasant but which you cannot quite place.

Or, you muse, it's the people. They're just….odd.

I had one such experience. Well, perhaps I've had many of these experiences to a lesser degree, certainly during my formative years when my parents took my younger sister and I away on holiday to some very strange locales. But this one. Oh boy, this one was real, so very real. So intense, so emotional, so unsettlingly *surreal* that it changed my life. Forever.

You see, I'm a writer. Freelance. I write for just about anyone and anything. I've been doing it since I left school with an A level in creative writing and it's kept me afloat ever since; a situation which was helped ever so slightly after my parents passed and left me with the few scraps of inheritance that they had tucked away for a forthcoming rainy day. I've written for the local rag, scribed for a few glossy magazines and now, with everything digitised and virtualised, I provide blog submissions for websites. Online publications in just about any topic and just about any country. I'm the literary equivalent of a jack of all trades, not particularly awesome at anything, but pretty damn good at most things. Or, at least, that's what I tell myself and, by the way, my bank balance seems to agree.

It was two years ago, the summer of 2017. The days were long and hot, the nights were sweaty and sticky and during one of those sleepless, uncomfortable evenings while I was between jobs and spending fruitless time on my 'labour of love' crime novel, '*The Drowning of Alice Bigsby*', one of my occasional employers, Travel Bug, messaged me and asked me to take a trip down to a little village on the South West coast of England and write a review of their local festival, the hunt for Lord Evreux. Bemused, I looked it up. As I had suspected it was one of those west country things where the local hicks get dressed up in medieval garb and chase some other oddly dressed villager around the cobbled and narrow streets with sticks and fake swords while other's bang drums, cheer and chant, dance to gaelic music, eat pies and pasties and drink copious amounts of real ale. It sounded right up my proverbial street and so I accepted with pleasure.

It was a long drive, seven hours in all, and by the time I arrived at the bed and breakfast, the 'Lucky Traveller' no less, I was tired and more than a little grouchy. The traffic had been horrendous; once you left the motorway the roads, if you could call them that, were slow, windy and not very smooth and the suspension on my little Fiat 500 had taken one hell of a battering. As had my backside. I hauled in my sports holdall containing my belongings and rang the bell.

'Good day sir, welcome to Fey. How was your trip?' The old lady was short, with long silvery hair and a narrow, snow white face.

'Hi, yeah. It's good to be here at last. My trip was not the best I'm afraid but,' I sighed wearily, 'I'm here now and that's all that matters. The name's Deacon, I have a booking.'

She smiled at me through thin, pastel pink lips and flipped through her tattered diary.

'Deacon, Deacon. Ah, there you are. Frederick. I'm Madgy, short for Madgy,' she grinned, 'pleased to meet you,' she offered her hand and I shook it swiftly, 'you're in for the weekend?' She eyed me up and down as if inspecting a filly at market.

'It's Freddy, nice to make your acquaintance,' although I had the peculiar feeling that we had met before, 'and that's right. I'm afraid you've got my company for the next three days, give or take.' I laughed. She didn't.

'Well that's good, that's very good,' she hopped down from her stool and reached behind her to the teak panel rack containing the room keys, 'we very rarely get people down here for more than a day or two. They seem to just,' she looked at me over her shoulder, 'move on. We're not really on the beaten track you see, a bit,' she turned and handed me my key, 'out of the way.'

'Thanks. Yes, you are a bit remote. Must be nice and quiet.' I looked at my key, the morticed deadbolt variety, and inspected the fob.

'Very quiet. Very peaceful. We have no trouble here.' She came round the counter, her head barely reaching my shoulders. 'No trouble at all,' she forced a vexatious smile, 'room three. Like the wishes. It's up the stairs and round to the left. Let me know if everything is to your,' she touched my hand and her fingers were trembling, 'satisfaction.' Her smile was real but her eyes gave away an anxious curiosity. I shook it off.

'Ok then. Thank you. I'm sure everything will be just fine.'

'Dinner's served from six. We have ox on this evening. It's been cooking all day. Just delicious. Be sure not to miss it,' she waddled back behind the counter.

'Right, ox. Sure. I'll certainly consider it.'

'Please do, and if you're going out this evening I recommend the Old Weasel. Serves a nice pint, if that takes your fancy, and the mead is outstanding,' she leaned over the counter top and leered at me, 'but watch out for Lord Evreux. He's crafty and he's mean and he'll be up to no good.'

I laughed, 'well I certainly hope I see him. That's why I'm here after all. You see I'm writing a review.'

'A review, a *review*,' she shook her head, 'well I'll tell you what I tell them every year,' she brushed her silver hair back behind her ears and stuck out a long, gnarly finger, 'keep your guard wary traveller and fetch your ear to the wind. The maidens are a-calling, their dance 'bout to begin. ' She threw her head back and gave out a shrieking, rasping and slightly unnerving howl of laughter.

*

I decided to try the pub. I'd never eaten ox (surely it was just tough beef) and I had no inclination to try it. What I really fancied was something with a bit of a kick; a chilli or a curry maybe. Something to wake me up after my long drive and reinvigorate my taste buds. My tongue felt as furry as a hair ball and my throat was bone dry. Unfortunately, when I took my seat, supped my first sip of the warm, thick, syrupy ale and checked the bar menu it was clear that all that was on offer was good old fashioned English fayre, straight out of Chaucer or Dickens. After some heavy sighs and a little solemn consternation I plumped for the suckling pig.

'That's a good choice sir. You won't be disappointed with that,' the landlord, a stout, white bearded man with a severe case of gout in his nose took my order with a wink and a smile, 'we gets 'em from old Bob up in the moors. Cooked slowly over a spit in the clay oven. Mother makes the gravy with her own secret recipe. She won't tell you what's in it you know? She'll keep that a secret until she departs this mortal coil, you mark my words.'

I smiled at the west-country caricature standing in front of me and considered how I would fit him into my review. 'Sounds delicious. I can't wait to try it.'

He tucked his pencil behind his ear and paused. 'That doesn't sound like a Cornish accent, sir. May I ask where you're from?' The old fella considered me with a curious eye. He had the air of a man that liked to take on copious amounts of information.

'I travelled from Kent this morning. A long journey I'm afraid,' I took a hefty swig from my ale.

'Kent, eh? A Kentish man,' he ran a gnarled hand through his wiry beard, 'we have a man of Kent here boys! A visitor from the east!' The locals set their ales and other assorted alcoholic beverages down on their respective tables and looked across at me with suspicion and mistrust. 'A visitor from the other side of this fair country, a Cantium boy no less.'

A series of mumblings, sniggers and the occasional cuss emanated from the oddball crowd. I wasn't concerned or offended but I did feel that sense of unease you get when you walk into a part of town where you simply do not belong.

'Don't fret my boy, just a friendly bit of banter from your Dumnoni cousins,' he patted me on the shoulder hard, wiggled his bulbous, lumpy and painfully red nose and walked off, chuckling and muttering under his breath. I reached for my notebook and started scribbling.

When I looked up from my musings I saw her. Well, *them* actually but it was her that I was transfixed upon. She glided in as if upon jets of air from her heels, her platinum hair shining with a heavenly radiance as she shook it out from underneath the hood of her assorted rainbow patterned, woollen sweatshirt, her petite and pointed face exuding kindness, warmth, confidence and, above all, an unnatural beauty. She was five foot tall, no more, wore fingerless woollen mittens, a colourful skirt with unicorn adorned stockings underneath, rainbow socks and boots that would not have looked out of place on a building site. She carried a well-worn ruck sack that looked far too large for her slight frame and wore a necklace and several bracelets that appeared to be laden with charms, trinkets and various other adornments. She was unconventional for sure, but none of that could erase what could only be described as her effortless grace. I took a large gulp from my ale.

I watched as she grabbed a hold of her friends; one male, one female, both dressed in similar garb, and walked over to a table not far from mine. Two older men and a lady sat at the table, drinking beer and eating chunks of deep fried pig skin. They eyed her with curiosity. I decided to eavesdrop like any good journo.

'Well?' the lady of the group addressed the youngsters. She was dressed in a dark cardigan, her long, dark, scraggly hair falling around her plump face which was deeply mottled with the effects of too much cornish air and ale. 'What news? Did you see any trace of him?'

'We've been up at the mound,' it was the young boy that spoke first. He pulled the red and purple beanie from his head and ran a mittened and muddy hand through his shaggy, blonde locks, 'near Dozmary point. We looked all around. Young Briony from Mousehole said that he had been spotted there just last night.'

'Briony of Mousehole? She's hardly a trustworthy source, Pip. Her father is from Dartmoor,' this time the elder of the two gentleman spoke up. He had a long red and silver beard, a bald head and piercing blue eyes that seemed as though they could penetrate ballistic armour. He munched on his pork scratching as he spoke, spitting bits of pig skin all over the table. '*And*? Speak up younglings. What did you find?'

The boy looked at the girl with mousey hair and gave her a gentle nudge. She spoke quietly and reluctantly, 'there were blackberries. Lots of them. Hundreds, maybe thousands,' she was visibly agitated as she spoke, her hands undoubtedly shaking from a concoction of the cold air outside and her obvious trepidation, 'crushed and trampled, brambles scattered this way and that, the ground underfoot was churned like curds. And the juice,' she gulped, 'the juice was running along the path like ox blood.'

I stifled a giggle.

The second gentleman at the table gripped his tankard in both hands, 'this is a bad omen indeed,' he shook his head, atop of which he wore a black, wide-brimmed walker's hat. He too had a beard but it was of the wiry, catweazle variety, the moustache waxed and looped, the beard long and thin. 'It appears we really do have *him* in our midst.'

'*Lets* not jump to any unnecessary conclusions Jacca,' it was the lady who swiftly and desperately interjected, 'this is not *proof*. There is no proof here,' she laughed a shrill, almost maniacal but unconvincing laugh.

'But Izzy says they saw blackberry juice. *Crushed* blackberries,' Jacca continued to shake his head, his hat tilting from side to side like a vessel lost at sea, his hands gripping onto his tankard of warm liquid so tightly that his knuckles were pure white, his face ashen, 'it is as it has always been. As we have foreseen for centuries. As the *fable* describes it!'

I struggled to control myself with the hilarity of it all but managed to keep it together. I couldn't wait to get it down on paper.

'Now, now Jacca,' red beard interjected, 'there could have been a deer up there, or a boar. Even a bunch of kids. Some squashed fruit does not prove that *he* is upon us,' he grabbed Jacca's arm, 'we've had this kind of false start before. *Don't you remember '82*? We had the whole village chasing shadows for weeks. And for what? Because some outsider had come in and decided to start their own unregistered fruit and veg' patch,' he laughed reassuringly, 'this is hardly beyond reasonable doubt, man.'

The boy grabbed the platinum haired angel's hand. 'Tell them Gwenora,' he kissed her on the forehead, 'tell them what you saw,' his eyes implored her to speak, '*you must.*'

Gwenora smiled at the boy, placed a delicate, white hand on his cheek and nodded. When she spoke it was as soothing and as beautiful as a dawn chorus, as sweet as the lilting sound of a children's church choir at

Christmas. My cynicism all but evaporated in the warm, scented breeze of her voice. 'I saw him Mariot, Jacca, Petroc,' she looked at each of them in turn, from the lady, to wide hat, to red beard, 'I saw him, in all his benevolent glory. And you need to mark my….*our* words,' she smiled a fierce, steadfast smile, '*he* is coming.'

*

There aren't many places in Kent that can claim they have their own resident druid but the west-country counties, Cornwall in particular, are full of them. Just look it up. A quick google count will get you well into the hundreds in Devon, Cornwall and Somerset alone. And sure enough, during the prior evening's events at the Old Weasel, events which had left me perplexed, amused and more than a little in love, I had spotted, pinned to a tatty old cork noticeboard, a yellowing, faux parchment flyer extolling the skills and virtues of the great druid Catuvellaunus (I dare you to attempt the pronunciation). I had taken a photo of the address on my smartphone and decided to visit the following morning.

Having had a hasty breakfast of thick bacon and yolky goose egg at the 'Lucky Traveller' I slung my world weary rucksack over my shoulder and headed out.

Catuvellaunus' dwelling was only a short ten minute walk up the hill and I paused periodically to view the stunning views out towards the bay. The coastline was just beautiful; the small cove sweeping from east to west, bordered by an ancient granite block and moss and lichen infused wall, several colourful and impressively crooked cottages, busy taverns and small, family run hotels, vistas of silver birch, hazel and hawthorn with great swathes of green foliage overhanging the granite cliffs like orc fingers stretching and reaching for the hidden treasures of the ocean. Various assortments of gulls, crows and birds of prey swooped and swooned for attention over the landscape, all competing in the great hunt for morsels of field mice, voles, young rabbits and chunky seaside chips. Wannabe surfers scoured the coastline in tight fitting bodysuits, carrying compacted foam body-boards adorned with pictures of coral sea-life or leaping dolphins while wearing luminous beech shoes and necklaces containing sharks teeth and prehistoric bones. The place took me back to my childhood; crab fishing all day with my dad and my little sister, eating greasy battered cod out of a polystyrene tray, battling the gale force winds and sideways rain and returning home with snotty noses and icy cold bodies. Maybe I had started off on the wrong foot with the village of Fey, I pondered. Maybe my weary disposition had gotten the better of me.

The hill was steep and my energy levels were low, but I panted and puffed my way along several winding streets and alleyways to the address on my phone. Number 13, Heaven's Gate. The short cul-de-sac contained just four bungalows, the most dishevelled of which belonged to the infamous druid. I opened the crooked gate and walked up the overgrown, mulchy path to the front door, it too in need of some immediate care and attention. I tapped loudly.

When the door opened I was taken aback. Maybe I had some preconceived opinion of what a druid should or would look like. I had half expected a Gandalf come Merlin hybrid with a long wispy beard, shaggy white hair, long robe and maybe even a pointy hat. What I got was a man of around six feet in his late twenties with smartly combed dark hair, thick spectacles, button down polo top and slacks. He looked more like a banker than a medieval soothsayer.

'Sorry, I'm…er,' I looked him up and down and then at the number on the door, 'I was looking for the druid. Druid Catuvellaunus?' I pronounced the name with care.

'That is I,' he looked down at me from his elevated position and frowned, 'you wish to have a reading?'

'A reading?'

'Cards, palm, *tea-leaves*?' He eyed me with an undisguised look of distaste.

'Er, no. Nothing like that all.'

'A séance? A play at the Ouija-board?

I was perplexed, 'no, no. Just a chat. You see,' I flashed my ID, 'Freddy Deacon's the name. I'm a writer and I'm writing a piece on the festival. Of Lord Evreux? It's for the Travel Bug. You know? The online…'

'That's good,' he ushered me inside, looking over my shoulder and up and down the cul-de-sac as he did so, 'because I don't do readings, séances and the like and neither does any self-respecting druid. But, *oh no*,' he waved his arms theatrically, 'apparently that's all these idiots are interested in. Can you tell me if I'm going to have a long life? Can you contact the dead cousin of my best friend's boyfriend's ex-girlfriend? Can you help me win the bloody Lotto?' He grabbed me by the arm and looked at me solemnly, 'can you imagine the indignity?'

'I…I guess not,' I walked into a narrow, dimly lit hallway, within which were littered several rows of pots and trays growing what can only be described as exotic herbs.

'But an interview? For an online magazine?' he pushed a big hand through his neat side parting, 'that I can accommodate.'

The druid closed the door behind him and walked past me into the living room. 'Come on in, sit,' he ushered me to a brown leather sofa and passed me a cup and a saucer. He smiled a big beaming smile, all teeth and gums, and proffered, 'tea?'

I settled myself into the large sofa and took the cup, 'er...yes please. That would be great. Milk and two...'

'No, no, *no* dear sir. No milk, no sugar. This is a tea of the herbal variety. None of that factory sealed, mass produced rubbish,' he poured a dark, fragrant liquid into my cup, 'dandelion, rose hip and root ginger to be precise,' he filled my cup to the brim, 'it's home- made but be careful, it has a kick.'

I raised the cup to my lips and took a sip of the warm, sweet but bitter liquid. It hit the back of my throat like cheap after shave on an open wound. I shuddered and blinked both eyes rapidly. He laughed as if he had just played an intricate but satisfying practical joke on me.

'Good isn't it?' he poured himself a cup, 'very good for the constitution and,' he took a long sip and looked me up and down with earnest sincerity, 'it will also aid your sense of smell.'

I set my cup down and withdrew my notebook from my bag.

'I wanted to ask you about the festival.'

'Lord Evreux?'

'Yes, that, but also about a conversation I overheard last night which has intrigued me.'

The druid sipped eagerly from his tea and leant back into the arms of his tattered and worn reading chair, 'and where did you hear this conversation?'

'At the Old Weasel.'

He scoffed, 'a den of gossip and spite if ever there was.'

'Yes, well, I couldn't comment on that, but the conversation was in reference to a person that some locals were looking for. I assume it was the Lord, or somebody playing the part of that character, but they seemed afraid, concerned.'

The druid withdrew his spectacles from his eyes and pinched the bridge of his nose between his index finger and his thumb. 'This festival gets more peculiar every year I'm afraid. You,' he put his spectacles back on and peered at me, 'you have heard of the legend of Lord Evreux I assume?'

I shrugged, 'a little, but I really had very little time to carry out any research prior to my trip.' I lied. I had had plenty of time but I'm afraid I am what is known as a lazy researcher. I tend to pick it up on the hoof. I'd managed to cope for so long that I really knew no other way.

'A tricky fellow in his day and one which has, unfortunately, been made infamous more by myth and legend then by actual fact and history.'

I scribbled in my book, 'how so?'

The druid set down his tea and stood, lighting thick candles and long joss sticks held in large, free

31

standing candelabras and the jaws of intricately ornate incense burners respectively, such items situated haphazardly around the small but uniquely furnished lounge. He pulled the shades across the front window and sat back down in his chair. The air immediately filled with the scent of cinnamon, honey and oriental spices.

'He was a devil of a man. A real charlatan. He was the lord of these lands, all of Fey and its surrounding countryside for five years or so back in the seventeenth century, but he treated the locals like slaves and the women like whores. He was born into a wealthy family and never worked a hard day's labour in his life but he expected the villagers to work day and night, ploughing the fields, manning the boats and brewing the ale. He increased taxes and enforced their collection with beatings and floggings. No-one, not one soul in the village, could stand the man.

'Four years after his father died, leaving him as his sole heir, legend has it that the Lord started to get lonely. He had never taken a wife and the only souls that lived with him in the sprawling Evreux House were his servants; cleaners, chefs, gardeners and the like, and not even they could stand to be in his company. And so, after many months of consideration, he decided to seek out and wed his one true love. Someone to settle down and start a family with. Someone to carry on the Evreux name. Someone to ensure that these lands stayed in the iron grip of the family for centuries to come. But he hadn't considered the hatred and loathing that the locals had for him and no matter how hard he tried; he held parties, social gatherings, events planned and constructed with the sole purpose of finding a mate, he was unable to coax even the poorest of the villagers to take him as a husband.

'Evreux started to get enraged, furious even, considering the refusal of any local woman to take his hand as a personal act of abandonment and a slight on his family name. He was rich after all, more wealthy than anyone in the village and with enough in the family funds to support several families many life times over. He couldn't believe that his wealth alone could not attract even the plainest of maidens. The more he dwelled on it the angrier he got, and the angrier he got the more spiteful he became. He spent his evenings, alone in his study, concocting a plan. A plan to get *his revenge.*'

I put down my pen and took another sip from my tea. Despite the shocking aftertaste, combined with the scent of the candles and the ambience of the room it really was quite pleasant. 'I'm intrigued. Tell me about this plan.'

The druid waved incense smoke towards him, closed his eyes, inhaled deeply, and continued.

'It really was devilish. Ingenious even. He took the guise of a young maiden, name of Lowenna, and gained employ at one of the taverns, 'The Jolly Sailor'.

It's now a Co-Op or a Spa or some such, but back then it was the busiest pub in the village. Lowenna was large, Evreux was six and a half feet tall and quite stout, but she was a pretty girl and she was very popular with the locals. Legend has it that she had affairs with some of the local men of influence but I'm not sure how true that is. After all, it wouldn't take long for them to realise that Lowenna was not all that she seemed. But what I can believe, as much as one can believe a myth which has been passed down for centuries by word of mouth alone, is that Lowenna befriended many of the women in the village and started a collective; a social committee for the women of Fey to hold gatherings and events where they could discuss their shared issues, create hobby groups, travel out of the village on outings and generally get away from the humdrum of their down trodden existences. Lowenna positively encouraged feminism centuries before it became a thing and she was dearly loved by all the women of Fey. Idolised even.

'But, as you and I now know, all was not as it seemed and Evreux was knees deep in a plan to exact his vengeance. On August the fifteenth, in the year of our lord fifteen hundred and seventeen, Lowenna organised a boat trip around the bay. The boat was a large, sea faring fishing vessel that Evreux leased out to a local company and almost all of the two hundred women of the village had agreed to take part. There was going to be food and drink on board, a music act, a magician, even a jester. The day was a complete sell out, it was warm and the sun was shining. It couldn't have been more perfect.

'Except, that is, for the devious Evreux who had rigged explosives to the hull of the ship and had allocated only one rowing boat, a boat that he could use to extract himself moments before the explosives tore a hole through the hull and sent all two hundred women to their deaths at the bottom of the bay. Evreux would have the ultimate revenge on the women of the village for their treachery and betrayal.'

I drained the last of my tea, set my cup down on a coffee table covered in a heavy mosaic patterned cloth and looked across at the druid through a thick haze. 'So, what happened next? I'm sure I would have heard of the village of Fey before if it was truly the location of the mass murder of two hundred innocent women, even if it was five hundred years ago.'

The druid leaned forward in his chair and pointed a long finger.

'This is the part that starts to become more fantasy than fact and you will need to bear with me. I'm not sure that I believe it myself but it is as the legend has it and I will recount it as such.'

I nodded, 'absolutely fine. I'm not here to judge. Just to report what I find.'

The druid sat back in his chair and smiled, 'then I will continue.

'There is an air in this village. A feeling, a sense, a *smell* even. Something that you will have noticed when you crossed the border from Penzance and made your way along the coast. A shift in the magnetic field you might say, as if you had crossed the equator. What was up is now down, what was left is now right.'

I shrugged.

'That's the magic. The magic of *Fey*.'

I smiled but held back a laugh.

'It's been here for thousands of years, perhaps since the dawn of man, perhaps even before. It comes from the land, the sea, the sky. It is all around us and we are all blessed with its presence. It is something unique to our village and something that we cherish daily.'

My head was down and I was frantically scrawling. I couldn't bear to look the druid in the eye for fear of giggling uncontrollably.

'Lord Evreux, for all the years that he and his family had resided in Fey, had never paid attention, never taken notice. Never once stopped and listened to the forest, stared at the horizon or even looked at the stars. Fey was different, Fey *is* different. It is a different place from a different world. And it protects its own.

'Two hours into the boat trip, when the wine was flowing, the food was being devoured and the music and dancing was in full swing Evreux, in the guise of Lowenna, made his way to the stern of the ship and onto the rowing boat. He withdrew his flint from the pocket of his blouse and was set to light the fuse, the fuse to detonate the explosives and send all aboard the ship to their watery graves.

'However, seconds before he could do the dreadful deed something stayed his hand. Something light and beautiful, something so delicate but strong, soft but firm, soothing but resolute. He looked up to see a face, the beautiful face of a maiden with soft skin and golden hair. A face that seemed to float above him as if flying, something so kind and genteel but with a hard and stone set determination.

'After a moment Evreux brushed the hand away and again set himself to strike his flint but, at the last second, something twisted his arm hard to the right, almost pulling his shoulder out of its socket, and sent him overboard into the water.

'Evreux was shocked and, despite being an excellent swimmer, struggled to float in the clothes he had worn in his Lowenna disguise. His dress caught in his heels as he thrashed his legs and his petticoat covered his face like a thick pillow case. He floundered in the water until he could shake off his over clothes, but even after his dress floated away like the discarded skin of an eel he was unable to fare any better. It felt as if something was pulling at his feet, dragging him down into the murky depths. He thrashed his arms and called for help but, with his dress gone and the make-up washed from his face, all aboard the ship could see him for who he really was and they could not find it in themselves to save him. He screamed at them, called them ungodly names and cursed them for all eternity but he was cast away and the heavy, unseen weights around his ankles pulled him down, down into the deep crevices of the ocean. His plan had failed and he would die a lonely and bitter man in the icy cold bay of the village of Fey, the village that could *never* love him.'

I sat back on the couch and sighed. I was starting to feel heady and longed for some fresh air. 'And that is the legend of Lord Evreux?'

The druid smiled, 'not quite. You see, so the legend goes, the Lord didn't drown in the deep after all, but was able to float to the surface and crawl along the mudflats at low tide, dragging himself onto the shore and

41

finding solace with a local witch, name of Morai the Unwashed. She allowed him into her hovel, fed him and took him on as her man slave. She taught him the ways of her witchcraft, which was an evil and malevolent fayre, loved him like he had never been loved and together they committed their souls to the cause of Beelzebub himself. In return for his eternal servitude she promised that she would help him gain revenge on the maidens of Fey and all of their ancestors thereafter, even if it took an eternity to do so.'

I chuckled, 'and the villagers have held a festival to celebrate the anniversary of that fateful day ever since?'

'Ever since, this year being a special one. The *five hundredth* anniversary no less. And the villagers never miss a trick for an ale or two, let me tell you.'

I laughed. The druid had been very helpful and I had taken enough notes to really pad out my review. I was very grateful, if a little light headed.

'Now,' he continued, 'about this conversation.'

I had very nearly forgotten about the events of the previous day. They seemed almost inconsequential now. 'Ah yes. Apologies, it had slipped my mind. It was,' I waved it away, 'nothing really. Just some locals in the pub talking about something they had seen. Something about,' I placed a finger on my chin as I recalled the exchange, 'blackberries. Crushed blackberries, somewhere on a mound near,' I checked my notes, 'Dozmary Point. Evidence of someone or something rummaging about in the bushes, and something else about juice running like blood. *Ox blood*. The locals seemed extremely concerned.'

The druid immediately stood. 'I'm afraid you must leave.'

I was taken aback. 'Leave? But…'

'You must leave *now*. My wife will be home imminently and she hates the smell of joss sticks. I will need to fumigate the house before she returns.' He was at the front door before I could collect my things.

'Okay, if you insist, but thanks for your help. I'll be in touch when I have my first draft. I…'

'No bother. I'm glad I could be of service, but I would appreciate it if you didn't keep in touch. It's just that, my wife…..you see….it's complicated.' He almost shoved me out into the street and I went tumbling along the path, barely staying on my feet.

'Complicated. What do you mean complicated?'

'And if I were you sir I would stay away from the Old Weasel, the mound at Dozmary Point and any talk of blackberries and blood.' He was sweating and his neatly combed hair was now pointing this way and that, 'in fact

I would finish up your review immediately and leave the village. Go back to your home in Kent, it will be much more peaceful there I'd wager with none of this crazy villager talk. You've got all that you need here, I'm sure. Good day.'

And with that my strange encounter with the Druid Catuvellaunus was over.

*

I saw her on the walk back. Gwenora, perched on the sea wall and gazing dreamily out at the gently swaying north-Atlantic ocean like a siren watching for passing ships. She was dressed in a hippy skirt, a light, lilac hoodie and flower patterned Doc Marten boots. She was drinking a bottle of water and munching on a bright red apple, her hair fluttering across her face in the gentle westerly breeze. She was most certainly the most beautiful thing I had ever seen and I couldn't help but be captivated. It was maybe twenty or thirty seconds before I realised that I had stopped dead in my tracks and was goggling at her like a whimsical teenager, too late to realise that she had turned her head and was looking straight back at me.

She waved me over and I sheepishly obeyed.

'You're not from around here are you?' Her voice sang to me like the most beautiful of orchestral ballads.

'No, I'm a visitor. Just here for a few days. It's my first time visiting your beautiful village.' I was over compensating like a fool.

'Not so beautiful I'm afraid, but thank you none the less. It has a history, this place, a very *old* history that affects us all in different ways. I, for one, would be happy to be anywhere else.' I hadn't spotted it before but a tear glistened on her cheek. She noticed me noticing and hastily wiped it away.

'Are you okay?' I sat down next to her on the sea wall, my legs dangling beneath me as the waves sloshed around and occasionally reached gallantly towards my stupidly young sports trainers as if the ocean was enquiring, *what are these things? Aren't you a little too old for these teenager shoes*? More correctly, I was probably too old for the radiant female sitting alongside me. I was in my thirties and she appeared to be no more than somewhere elusively in her twenties but I was hooked and enjoying our unexpected rendezvous.

'I'm fine', she smiled at me and my heart skipped several beats. Her expression was beaming, glowing and joyous and everything I had hoped for, 'just a little bit emotional.' She sniffed, wiped her nose on the back of her hand and grinned, 'I'm like that.' Her eyes shifted from right to left and she grabbed my hand, 'I don't know you Freddy but I sense you have a good soul. Will you be attending the festival tomorrow?'

I blinked at her. She knew my name. I didn't know how but the very sound of her harmonious voice speaking my name, as if we had been acquaintances all our lives, gave me goose bumps. 'Yes, I will be attending the festival. In fact, that's the very reason…'

'…you're here. I know.'

'How did you…?'

She put a finger to my lips and it tasted of butterscotch and something….bitter. I resisted the urge to open my mouth. 'It's of no consequence Freddy. Let's just say that I had an interest and so I found out. It's a small village after all and I know everyone. What do you think of my skirt?'

She leapt up onto the sea wall and twirled around, the colours in her striped tutu giving the illusion of a rainbow halo encircling her like the rings of Saturn. I looked down at the water and was suddenly very afraid that she might fall in.

'It's very nice. It suits you.' I blushed at the hilarity of such a forced complement. I simply didn't know how to speak to her. I'm a man whose words are his business and yet every word in the English language seemed to be failing me.

'Then I will wear it tomorrow. Make sure you're there early. There will be quite a show.' And then she bent, kissed me on the forehead and raced off towards the path that snaked around the cliff face towards the cottages above. The colours in her clothing seemed to shift and swirl like oil on the surface of water, sometimes dark and absorbing, sometimes bright and reflective. I was mesmerised and entranced by her, as if her very presence brought something back to my subconscious, something from a distant age. A feeling of warmth, comfort and simpler times. The feeling you get when you have a good meal of home cooked food in front of a roaring fire with a glass of something sweet and delicious.

And then with a flash and a flicker she disappeared behind the thick foliage. I touched a hand to my forehead and smelled the scent from my fingers. Strawberries. Or blackberries.

I didn't know what to make of the emotional whirlwind that was Gwenora but even after a few lonely pints and a single malt whiskey at the Old Weasel that evening, sleep avoided me. Her hypnotic face was seemingly emblazoned on the insides of my eyelids and I was unable to shake it.

*

I was out of bed early and went for a jog along the water front and up through the hills. It was a beautiful morning and the villagers were already out and about, putting up bunting, placing tables and chairs along the bay, setting up stalls selling various home-made produce and decorating the band stand ready for the stream of folk musicians that would be playing an assortment of stringed and percussive instruments during the course of the festival.

I waved and nodded as I jogged past the men and women at work and enjoyed the intensity of the run. The sweat that was forming on my face and the drum beat of my heart in my ears was providing a welcome distraction from the images racing through my head from the previous two days. Lord Evreux, the attempted drowning, Morai the Unwashed, the talk of Beelzebub, the blackberry juice running like blood through the hills, the frightened villagers, Gwenora, her beauty and her bewitching personality. How had she known who I was and what I did for a living? Was I that interesting to her? What had I said to the druid to make him react in such a way? What was it about his story that had me so intrigued? Why was this village and its strange but fascinating inhabitants having such a profound effect on my subconscious?

I had tried to get some of it down on paper during my sleepless night but, frankly, I didn't think any of it was publishable? I had resigned myself to getting as much detail as I could during the day's festivities and hoped that at least some of it would appear both sane and interesting to the dedicated Travel Bug subscriber.

I spotted the landlady from the 'Lucky Traveller', hamper in hand, trekking up the foothills away from the village and towards the forest. She looked preoccupied. Something seemed to be leaking from her hamper. I thought blood maybe, but I shook that idea off as the crazy suspicion of a lone reporter looking for a headline.

'Hey!, Hey Mrs…Madgy!' She turned and I put up a hand in greeting, keeping my stride and panting hard. It might just have been my deepening paranoia, I mused, but she looked afraid of something, as if I had given her an unwelcome start and, without acknowledging me, she turned back to face the way she was going and quickened her step. I didn't know the lie of the land and so had no idea where she was headed, but wherever it was she was off in a hurry. I decided to shrug it off.

A couple of hundred yards later I spotted one of the gentleman from the 'Old Weasel', Jacca. He had a large walking cane and was headed in a similar direction to the old lady. I hadn't been introduced and so didn't call to him, but what was of interest to me was the large bale of heather he had tucked into his rucksack. Not that unusual in Cornwall, heather being considered lucky, particularly by the Romany gypsy contingent, but his demeanour, looking over his shoulder as if fearful of being followed, was an oddity that stood out a mile. I jogged on but I was becoming ever more curious. I decided to ask Gwenora later that day whether there was a more secretive festival occurring in the forest located in the hills above the village and, if that were true, attempt to blag myself an invite. The addition of an underground, less touristy element to the Festival of Lord Evreux would make for an excellent addendum to my review.

I coasted back down the incline, nodded to the young girl standing in at reception at the 'Lucky Traveller' and returned to my room for a shower and a change of clothes.

As I opened the door and stepped inside I almost choked on my own saliva. There was a basket of fresh, plump blackberries placed neatly on my bed. I felt my warm blood turn positively arctic and the hairs on my arms and neck stand on end. I stepped closer and spotted a card with a hand written, cryptic note, simply stating;

I look forward to seeing you this evening. We will again dance the dance of the maidens of Fey.

I held the card closer to my nose, grabbed my reading glasses and peered at the tiny post script underneath.

PS. Watch out for the Piskies. They will only seek to thwart us.

*

After enquiring whether anyone, other than the staff members, had access to my room I put the gift down as a bizarre prank by the irksome Madgy. I assumed it was all part of the fake ambience required to draw unsuspecting visitors into the mythical mood of the festival and I decided to jump in feet first and go with it. When I saw her later in the day I would play along with the joke and beat her at her own game.

The day kicked off at eleven o' clock with music from a banjo, acoustic guitar and bongo band called 'The Bumpkins of Bedlam' and there was much jigging, dancing and general frivolity. There were dozens of stalls selling all sorts of produce and delicacies. Hot pasties and various assortments of sausage rolls, home crafted clothing, hand-made pottery of all shapes, colours and sizes, pickles, jams, cooking sauces and honey from the local bee hive farm, hand stitched moccasins, belts made from locally farmed cow hide, ornaments and trinkets, ales brewed in the village and wine mashed by the feet of the maidens of Fey. There were several hand stuffed caricatures of the infamous Lord Evreux scattered around the sea front and the locals took turns in bashing him, hanging him, disembowelling him and generally abusing the poor fellow. Docked in the shallow beech was a replica of the fishing boat that the good Lord used in his attempted mass drowning, complete with fake explosives and cardboard cut outs of the maidens of Fey themselves. You had to hand it to the villagers. They didn't do things by halves.

I bought myself a pint of Furry Fey and a pork, sage and apple sausage roll and wandered along the street, perusing the stalls and nodding my head to the music. Half of me was mentally taking notes for my review and the other half was looking out for a platinum haired beauty named Gwenora. I took a seat at a wooden bench outside the 'Old Weasel', nodded at the landlord who was outside serving up lashings of barbeque and hot drinks to passing spectators, and crowd watched. It really was a beautiful day and, as the Bumpkins of Bedlam gave way to a female fiddle and guitar group called Faeries Gift and they in turn gave way to a six piece folk group of what could only be described as hairy old blokes (aptly called the Hairy Oiks), I began to lose faith that Gwenora was coming at all. Lunchtime came and went, one pint turned into three and before I knew it the afternoon was behind me and the evening was approaching. It was time to drown the Lord.

Drowning the Lord, it turned out, was not as simple as it sounded. It involved the villagers dancing, conga style, from the sea front to the top of the hill to a ditty belted out by the Oiks, finishing at a large tent on the cliff edge where dark, thick and eye wateringly strong mead called the Lord Evreux was poured into paper cups for everyone in attendance. Simultaneously the locals hoisted an eight foot wooden statue of the man of honour to the front of the conga line, downed the mead in one (hence, drowning the Lord) and then hurled the figurine from the cliff into the dark and swirling tide below. All was done with a sense of humour and fun but I couldn't help but think it was all in particularly bad taste.

It was as I stood, softly swaying from side to side from the effects of my third pint of ale and considering the tone of my review and whether I would infuse my write up of the day's events with a sombre mood reflecting the banality of the Lord's brutal assassination, that I felt a soft and almost electrically charged tap on my shoulder. I turned and saw Gwenora, dressed in her rainbow skirt, tangerine hoody and a floral crown. She kissed me on the lips and she tasted of summer.

'Did you get my message?'

I licked my lips dreamily and half answered, 'Your….your what?'

'In your room.' She frowned at me, 'did you get my message?'

I was stunned back to reality. 'That was *you*?'

She laughed. 'Yes. Yes it was. Wasn't it *hilarious*?' She waved her arms from side to side and spun round and around like a delighted child. 'I thought I would have some fun.' She laughed and pointed at me, 'your face is a picture.'

I laughed, but honestly, I didn't find it funny. 'How…how did you get into my room?'

She tilted her head to one side. 'Oh Freddy,' she smirked, 'I have my ways.' She looked over at the amassed crowd. 'What did you think of….that?'

I decided to be honest. 'A bit brutal actually.'

'Barbaric even?'

'Yes, I guess so.'

'Well, that would make sense, given your....' she paused and placed a long finger on the dimple in her chin, 'past.' She winked and then turned and walked down the hill, back to the village.

'My what? Where...' I started to walk after her, 'where are you going?'

'Come on, hurry up.' She didn't break stride and was surprisingly nimble on her toes, 'I have something to show you.'

'Wait. I...,' I turned back to the dispersing crowd and muttered under my breath, 'my review...'

'This is for your review, silly,' she hollered, 'much more interesting than that nonsense.'

I decided to concede and followed her like a love sick puppy. I couldn't believe that she had actually kissed me. I felt dizzy from the emotion of it all.

We passed through the village and up the hill, passed the 'Old Weasel', the 'Lucky Traveller' and through the winding streets that I had jogged along that very morning. I looked behind me at the slowly setting sun, its reflection laying on the calm water below like a red velvet blanket. The next band was in full swing and the throng had returned to the sea front, the evil Lord banished to the depths and the village maidens once again safe from his dastardly clutches. I couldn't believe that they did this every year. I admired their conviction, if not their methods.

We left the cottages and bungalows behind us and headed along a dirt track, across a field of corn, up a further incline and into a thick copse of trees. The copse became a forest and the forest became very dark. We didn't need a torch as Gwenora seemed to emit light from her very being. It may have been the ale but she looked like an angel to me. An angel sent to redeem my soul and deliver me to absolution. I was well and truly under her magnificent spell and I was enjoying every second of it.

'Do you remember your childhood Freddy?' I was a few feet behind her and she spoke to me without turning, but I heard her as clearly as if the words were being spoken from inside my own skull.

'Yes. Most of it,' I smiled, 'it was a happy time.'

'Do you remember your parents? Your father? Your mother?'

'Yes. They were wonderful people.' I loved my parents and missed them deeply.

'How did they die?'

'I…,' I paused and considered my answer, 'I…I can't remember.'

'That's odd isn't it?' It was and I felt confused. Maybe it was the effects of the beer. I walked after her.

'I'm sure I'll remember when I...,' I shook my head as if trying to dislodge the memory, 'when I have a clear head.'

'Do you remember your sister?'

'Of course.' These questions were confusing and pointless and beginning to annoy me. All I really wanted was to hold Gwenora in my arms and feel the warmth of her skin against mine.

'Do you remember how *she* died?'

I was horrified, 'died? What do you mean died?' I was furious and sickened all at once, 'my sister is alive and well and doing just fine thank you very much.'

Gwenora continued her march uninterrupted and never once turned her head to address me. She simply asked, 'are you sure?'

I stopped dead in my tracks, as if someone had pulled at a loose thread and my legs had come away from my body like those of a discarded rag doll. I felt the blood run from my face and the energy pour out of me like water from a leaky bucket. I wasn't sure. I wasn't sure at all.

She continued unperturbed. 'Do you remember your maternal grandmother?' I stood stock still, reeling from the revelations that were falling from the holes in my fractured memory.

'I do.'

'Do you remember her family name? From before she was wed?'

I strained my memory, desperate to find something in there that rooted me back to my previous preconceptions of where I came from.

'Heather….Heatherall I think?'

'Heatherall. Yes. That's it. And your mother was an only child?' Gwenora had stopped walking but still faced away from me.

'Yes. I believe she was. Look, Gwenora, what is all this ab....'

'Do you remember when your parents brought you to Fey, when you were a young boy?'

A memory crept back into my head like a bug. 'Yes....I believe I do.' It was the summer of 1994 and I was around ten years old. My sister would have been eight. She was so beautiful and I adored her. So did my parents. They called her their little angel and I agreed. She had bright platinum hair, white skin, an impish face and long skinny fingers. I felt something click inside of me but I couldn't make the connection. I was still revelling in my long, lost, but recently returned memory.

We had spent long days on the beach, swimming in the low tide and playing in the rock pools, looking for

65

crabs and tiny fish. We had candyfloss, lemonade, fish and chips for supper and my dad would eat jellied eels which my mum found disgusting. She called them elephant bogies. The English weather would give us sun burn and wind chills in equal measure and we would be smeared from head to toe in thick sun cream and then covered up in all in one swim suits and cardigans. And we had an inflatable dinghy. A yellow one with a red stripe. The thought of the dinghy caused me pain but, again, the connection escaped me.

'We have missed you Freddy. You've been gone a long time but we are glad that you have returned. Do you know where you are standing?'

I didn't. It was dark and the only light was that emitting from Gwenora and her tangerine hoody. I looked around me but could only make out faint, dark shapes. Suddenly and inexplicably a fire erupted between

Gwenora and I. It illuminated my surroundings with an immediacy that was both jarring and welcoming.

I was in a clearing, deep in the forest, standing in the middle of a thick grouping of brambles. Hundreds of blackberries hung from the thorny, snake like arms, and, when I looked down at my feet I saw that I was standing in several hundred crushed berries, the juice pooling around my shoes like the blood of a hunted animal. And, horrifyingly, tied and gagged to wooden stakes situated in each of the four corners of the clearing were Mariot, Jacca and Petroc, the three villagers who were drinking at the 'Old Weasel' during my first night in the village, and the old landlady, Madgy. All four looked terrified and, I felt sure, more than a little ashamed. None of them would look at me.

'Do you know these people Freddy?' Gwenora had turned to face me but she was obscured by the roaring camp fire.

'Yes I do. Why are they tied up? How did they get here? We need to release them.'

'Do you remember what they did? What they did to you and your family?'

I reached back into my deepest, darkest vaults and saw a flicker of something. The faces of the four people in front of me; younger, leaner, vibrant.

'You see Freddy. Over time names change, they evolve to suit the dialect of the era. Mispronunciation, misspelling or simply the deliberate altering of the name to make it easier to record or recollect. Over time names change significantly.' I was looking at each of the individuals in turn, frantically clawing at my memory banks to unveil the story that was hidden within. 'Heatherall, yes. Not so different to Evreux when you think of it.'

Petroc's eyes were imploring me for compassion, I could see it. He knew. He knew what the connection was. They all did. *Why didn't I?*

'These good people couldn't bear for an ancestor, a *male* ancestor, to carry on the legacy for fear of repercussions. It has been this way for centuries. Every male descendant has been culled, eliminated, *executed*, all in the name of the maidens of Fey. Folly, pride and superstition contrive to drive these good people to justify *murder*.'

I recalled the dinghy, my sister and I. Or was it Gwenora and I. No, it couldn't have been. My father was closer to shore, splashing my mother with icy cold sea water. We were drifting out to the open sea but we didn't care, the water was still shallow and we could both swim. My sister, Gwenora (yes, that *was* her name) would splash around and spin the dinghy, making ourselves feel sick and excited all at once. The sun was beaming down and the water was as blue as you like. There was a ripple and a motorboat. Four occupants. There was a hand on the dingy and a tug. We were dragged further out, past the edge of the cove and into the ferocious water beyond. Gwenora was frightened, she grabbed my arm. I held onto her and I could see the faces of the four on the boat. They were sad. One of the women was crying but the men scorned her. The hand holding the boat was that of the other woman, the short woman with the silvery hair. She had pity in her eyes but she was unyielding. She waved as she set us free and mouthed 'sorry'. I looked back at the shore and could see the faint outlines of our parents but they hadn't spotted us. Within seconds the heavy waves had overturned our dinghy and I was under. The current was too strong and I couldn't hold onto my beautiful, darling Gwenora. She pleaded to me as she was dragged down into the dark and terrifying depths but I was only ten years old and I couldn't swim to her, I didn't have the strength or the lung capacity. I sobbed and gulped down salty and foamy sea water and then all went black. I awoke on the shore, further along the coastline, with no idea how I got there, and my parents were holding me. My mother was sobbing and wailing and I knew something terrible had happened. I was right and it eventually drove my parents to oblivion. Less than ten years later they would be found in the garage of our home, the car engine running and a hose pipe through a crack in the window.

There was a shrill laugh from behind the flames.

'It was I who saved you that day Freddy, just as it was I who saved your great ancestor, my love.' Around the fire walked a tall, dark haired woman. Not the demure princess that lured me there in the guise of my beautiful and, I reluctantly recalled with deep remorse, long dead sister. No, this was a broad, statuesque brunette in a thick slate grey cloak and crooked black hat. Black, imposing eyes peered out from under the un-trimmed, ebony

71

eyebrows of a woman who was neither old nor young, neither ugly nor beautiful. The face of a woman who had a long story to tell and demons to exorcise.

I took three steps back, away from the scorching flames, 'you are…'

'Morai. That would be correct, although the unwashed tagline was added by the local rag-tags for their own amusement.'

'But that would make you…'

'Very old, yes. For mortals. Not so old for an immortal, however and I can assure you that my resolve has not wavered with the passing of time and I guarantee to you that we shall have our vengeance,' she held out her right arm and surveyed our surroundings, 'you will note the blackberries. *He* has visited us and he is standing with us, arm in arm.' She tilted back her head, opened her black lips and screeched a shrill and piercing laugh. Each of the captives visibly shuddered.

'I don't understand. Who is standing with us and why the blackberries?'

Morai walked towards me and took my hands in hers. Her touch was as cold as a shard of ice and as sharp as a thousand needles. 'Don't you see? I took the guise of your sister, Freddy, to comfort you and to ease you along your journey. Waking you from such a terrible amnesia, brought on by what these awful people did to you and your family, was a delicate and tricky affair. I did not want to damage you or weaken you in some irreversible way. We have much work to do.' I didn't understand. She saw the bemused look on my ashen face and gazed deeply and compassionately into my eyes. 'Your ancestor and I were lovers, he was my underling, my servant. He worshipped me, as any human should worship a *magnificent* immortal such as I. He helped me in my work and I in turn gave him the bloodline that he desired.' I looked at her, aghast, 'your *bloodline* Frederick,' she grinned at me through blackened teeth.

'My son spawned a son, and he in turn, and then he in turn and on and on until...,' she ran a hand down my face and I felt icicles instantly form in my veins, 'well, here we are,' she turned to look at each of her prisoners, '*back where we belong!*

I looked from Petroc, to Jacca, to the landlady, the very woman that had cast my sister and I asunder, and then to the terrified Mariot. 'Why?' I pleaded with them, '*why would you do this to us?*'

Morai answered, 'because you returned, Freddy. Your mother made the dreadful mistake of believing that, after all this time, the curse was lifted. But these folk are vengeful and hateful and they passed the message down through generations. They would never let an Evreux male back onto these lands for fear that he would seek his vengeance on the maidens of the village and complete the task that your great, great, great, *great* grandfather had set upon enacting. But they had presumed you dead, that both you and your sister had perished in the deep. They had not paid any mind to old Morai. Not reckoned upon my genius, on my *power*. That perhaps I would intervene. They didn't realise that I would *never* let you come to any harm. When you returned to Fey their guards were down. They didn't know,' she laughed a spiteful, sneering laugh, 'the imbeciles. But *I* knew. I have been watching you every day for decades. Watching and waiting. Waiting for this time, five hundred years to the very day. It was *I* that placed the call to your employer. It was *I* that requested you and you alone. And when I saw you that night in the Old Weasel I almost broke down. Here you were. Back with me. *Back in the bosom of your family.*' She reached for me but I stepped away, almost tumbling into the clawed, beckoning spikes of the blackberry vines. I reached out a hand to steady myself and tore the flesh between my thumb and my forefinger.

'For God's sake, what's with all the fruit?' I went to wipe my hand but Morai grabbed it and sucked deeply on the blood. I almost vomited. She smiled at me with my crimson life juice still settled on the surface of her cracked and blackened lips.

'Blackberries, my dear, are what bring *him* to us. They are the devils fruit and he is drawn to them. It is why after the late summer months these feeble humans no longer eat such delicacies. They consider them tarnished, tarnished with the foul deeds of hell,' she licked her lips, 'but we know them for what they are. They are the prize that brings the demon to us. That draws him out from the cracks in the rock, soil and human detritus, up from the fiery furnaces of hades, through the black, enchanted forest and out onto this sacred mound. The mound where your ancestor and I forged our magnificent, beautiful and *eternal bond.*'

She raised her cane and swept it through the base of the fire, shooting hot ash around the clearing and into the faces of the four shackled captives. 'All we need is the sweet and bitter juice of the sacred fruit,' she grabbed a handful of blackberries in her left hand, thorny vines intact, and squeezed; the mixture of juice and her own blood oozing through her fingers, 'the true and sweet essence of an Evreux heir,' she grabbed my wounded hand and pinched the flesh. I hollered but she squeezed all the more, my blood trickling down her long, bony arm. Over her shoulder, in the darkness, I saw the crimson, malevolent eyes of a beast, a horned, raging beast full of spite, hate and sordid anticipation. 'And the soul of a commoner. A filthy soul of a mortal with nothing to give to the world but its own greed, lust, vanity and desire to destroy. And *you*,' she pointed at each of them in turn, '*you* will provide me with the very soul I need!' She spat the words out with hatred and wickedness. 'Now which one will it be?' She gesticulated from left to right, grinning maniacally at each of the terrified, but belligerent, faces.

'Eeny, meeny, miny, mo', catch a filthy human by it's toe. If it hollers let it burn in the *raging fires of hell, ha ha ha!* Eeny,'

Jacca.

'Meeny,'

Petroc.

'Miney,'

Madgy.

'Mo.'

She screamed into the black night, a blood curdling, terrifyingly, ear splitting scream, and swung her cane towards the head of Mariot who howled for mercy through her sodden and soiled gag.

But just then, as Mariot was about to lose everything tangible from the neck up and the beast was ready to leap from its hiding place, no doubt to devour us all in an uncontrollable frenzy, two luminous shapes flew down from the tree tops and knocked the cane from Morai's determined grasp. She yelped in shock and reached for the cane, simultaneously stumbling forwards into the searing flames of the camp fire. She was completely engulfed, the tip of her hat just visible over the top of the highest burning flare, her arms flailing wildly in the midst of the inferno.

I was torn. Torn by what the four wretched individuals before me had done to my family, but also by my own internal compass which generally pointed north to humanity and compassion. I rarely went south but I had visited once or twice.

I watched as things I can only describe as imps in pointed hats or some such flittered around the four of them, untying their binds and kissing them gently on the cheeks and foreheads. I watched as Morai thrashed and flailed in the midst of the inferno. I watched as the horned beast receded back into the darkness, its disappointment obvious but its evil clearly undeterred. I watched as the imps, no *piskies*, approached me and eased back into their human forms; the awkward, gangly and scruffy Pip and the nervous but sweet natured Izzy. It seemed an eternity ago that these two had been at the 'Old Weasel' with Morai in the guise of Gwenora. Had they known all along?

'And you sir.,.' it was the boy who spoke first. 'You must leave and never, *ever* return. If you do this and swear that you will stay away then we will spare you. This is a good place and there is inherent evil within you. Evil that cannot be cleansed.'

'Let us finish what we came here to do. We have just one opportunity to rid the world of this evil sorceress and we must strike while she is weak.' Izzy, with the mousey brown hair and dark, sumptuous eyes, had the wreath of heather in her right hand and a bloody heart in the other. The heart of an ox, no doubt, carried to the mound in Madgy's hamper that very morning.

Petroc and Jacca were eyeing me warily and Mariot and Madgy were hugging each other tightly, seemingly terrified that I might wreak a brutal vengeance upon them.

'I am good, you don't know me. *I am a good person. There is no evil in me!*' I shouted above the deafening shrieks and screams still emanating from the burning witch.

'You are an Evreux, child,' the old lady let go of Mariot and walked forwards, 'an *Evreux*! Evil runs deep in your veins, *in your blood*! You cannot escape it, just as we cannot escape the magic of this place. It is within you and around you, it is inseparable.' She reached out her short, spindly arms, her fingers drawn towards my eyes as if ready to gouge them from their deep sockets. I started to pull away.

'Step back Madgy, you *old hag!*' Morai, stepped out of the inferno, her skin black and blistered, her hair still ablaze and her face a mask of smouldering flesh. She screamed and swung what remained of her scorched cane, cracking the old lady on top of her head with a swift and decisive motion. Blood trickled between Madgy's shocked and bewildered eyes as they rolled up into her skull. She fell to the floor hard.

The piskies were upon the witch as she threw off her burning cape. Morai turned to me and I could see her yellow and black eyes beneath her charred skin. 'Finish her my child! Finish the murdering crone. *Finish all of them*! Complete the spell and you will avenge your family!'

Petroc stepped forward, his red beard glistening in the ferocity of the now ravenous blaze. 'No, don't do it Freddy! She did, *we did*, what we had to do to save our village. We're sorry for what happened to your family but we only did it for the good of our people! What happened to your sister was a terrible, *terrible accident. Can't you see that?'*

Morai waved her left hand towards him almost incidentally and he flew back with the force of some invisible blow, smashing into the base of a tree. She turned to me as a piskie dug the prongs of its iron fork into her blackened face. 'Do it, Freddy! Do it now!'

I looked down at Madgy's peaceful form and felt sorrow. As blood pooled around her head I thought of my mother and father. What would they have me do? I thought about my beautiful sister, her smile, her laugh, the dance she did every morning when I sang to her. What would she make of all of this, what would she say if she were standing there with me, surveying the chaos that was occurring all around us? How would she guide me?

I closed my eyes and sought direction from my ancestors as Morai and the piskies, Pip and Izzy, danced the battle dance of the maidens of Fey.

*

Two years have passed and what happened that night occupies my thoughts every single day. The haunting memories of my sister slipping into the deep, the depression that ravaged my mother and father, my being taken away by foster parents and passed from family to family….those long forgotten images follow me around like storm clouds overhead, always just out of sight but casting their shadows nonetheless.

They say time is the greatest of healers and that is true to a degree. Every day I've felt a little better, every night I've slept a little longer. I look out at the sea and hope my sister's spirit is intact, riding the waves like a great galleon, her hair billowing behind her like a platinum mane, her smile, like a beacon, lighting the way ahead for lost travellers. I know that she is with me and that she is proud.

I have a home now. A home of my own. A happy place. A place where I feel that I belong. My writing has never been better and the work keeps pouring in. I do less of the travelling now. I've learnt my lesson.

I laugh a lot, to myself mostly, and I've learnt to draw pencil sketches. Mainly of what I saw; the eyes, the horns, the teeth. And what *he* did…after. It keeps me occupied and every now and then I smile. Contented.

As long as I do my chores, come when my mistress calls and keep the men at the village in check then…well, happiness reigns at Duzmory Point.

It turns out there's only one maiden of Fey after all, and they call her Morai the Unwashed.

Only By Night

I'm awake. It's early but I've got a lot of things to do and besides Caitlyn likes her tea and her low fat, low sugar, arid desert-sand muesli served to her in bed before she leaves for work. I sit up, rub a rough palm across my heavy eyes and breathe out a long, hoarse yawn. It's been a long week and the really hard work hasn't yet begun. I look across at the half open doorway to the bathroom and the hot shower that beckons inside. It calls to me.

The water is steamy and invigorating. I wash my short cut, dark but greying hair and lather my face, remembering as I do so to shave off my four day old beard. Caitlyn hates the whiskers, proclaiming that they irritate her soft, thrice daily moisturised face every time that we kiss. And I need to be sharp. In more ways than one.

THE MAIDENS OF FEY & OTHER DARK MATTER

The bright OLED sign from the bar across the street blazes a purple hue along the bed as my wife lies still sleeping. Her blonde hair fans out like a crown of golden thorns around her petite head, her sleep mask hiding her pretty yet world-weary eyes beneath. She is indeed a beautiful woman. Too beautiful for this old charlatan. Too beautiful for the life we have had together.

I tie a damp towel around my waste and walk across the hallway to the kitchen. I fill the kettle and flick a switch, being careful to take note of the power gauge situated next to the cooker hood. Still enough in the tank to last until the end of the week, as long as we're not too frivolous with the kitchen appliances. At least that's what I tell Caitlyn. I grab two mugs from the cabinet and throw in teabags and some skimmed milk. She's been trying to get me to lose a few pounds since Christmas and, Lord knows, she's right. The office life does not agree with my body's natural inclination to settle all saturated fat around my backside and hips. I take a mental note to ramp up the exercise in the not too distant future.

I hear her roll over in bed as I stir the tea. My mind switches to the upcoming events later in the day. Day. Night. Whatever. There's a lot to get done in a very short space of time and some fine lines to tread. It's going to take effort, timing and patience. This day has been a long time in the making and I sure as hell am not going to be the one to let them down. Not me. Jenna and the kids deserve better and, goddam it, they're going to get it. I'd made a promise. A vow even.

'You okay hon'?' She's awake.

'Yeah sweetie, just in the kitchen making the tea. You want your usual or can I tempt you with eggs and bacon? I've got some wholemeal muffins too if you fancy pushing the boat out.'

I hear her push herself up onto her elbows and see the light from the bedside lamp shine across the narrow hallway. 'You tease. You know I can't. I'm meeting with the board of directors today and I need to look my best. These hips are my big sell.'

'Oh yeah,' I ape, 'I forgot that was today. Silly me.'

I reach across the sink, grabbing the sealed jar containing the sawdust she calls breakfast and pour it into a ceramic bowl. No milk. No sugar. No taste. I put it on a tray with her tea and carry it across to her, remembering to tighten my towel around my soft waste, lest I expose myself and put her off of her morning feast.

'You all set? It's such a big day for you. I wish I could be there to egg you on,' I smile at her and place the tray down softly on the bed.

She yawns, her eye mask atop her head. Her long arms, adorned by her heavily manicured hands, are outstretched, her silk night dress barely covering her slight breasts.

'Oh baby, you know that I would love for you to be there, but you're not authorised. If you clear the exam next month then maybe we can work in the same building and perhaps your hours will be a little more flexible.' She smiles at me dismissively and wipes her eyes with the backs of her hands.

I sit down next to her. 'Yeah, I guess. I'm pretty confident so we'll see. I sure hope I can do better than last time. I don't know. Those test scenarios really tense me up. Doesn't matter how hard I study, it just seems to fall out of my ears when I enter the room.'

She pooches. 'Hon', you'll be just fine. I've got every confidence in you, and so does mummy. We'll be egging you on, you can count on it. Mummy said to me just the other day that the only problem you have is confidence. You just need to…believe in yourself more. Just like I believe in you.'

She caresses my shoulder and I run my hand through her hair and kiss her on the cheek. She turns her head and softly kisses me on the lips. I respond and we share a passionate embrace. She smells good. Vibrant and exciting. It's such a shame. I push myself off of the bed, pulling the towel closed around my manhood as I do so.

'I've got to get moving. I've got an early shift and Robbie's on holiday. We're a man down and fifty percent up on workload. Feels like I'm pulling the weight of two men for most of the time. I'll be home at around five, maybe six.'

'Oh, why so late? I was going to invite the Braehmer's over for dinner.'

I turn as I pull on my jeans, 'babe, I just said. I'm over worked and under paid. That's the lot you bought into I'm afraid.' I give her my best Hollywood grin, 'look, I'll do my best to get home early. I'll give you a call and let you know as soon as *I* do.'

She shovels in a mouthful of dry nuts and oats, 'well, you'll be missing out on my sea bass and green Thai curry sauce. It's your favourite.'

I button up my shirt and lean in to kiss her forehead. 'There'll be plenty of nights and plenty of sea bass. Have a glass of champagne for me. You'll do great today.'

She sips her tea and offers me a cute wave of her long, violet-clawed fingers. 'Never any doubt sweetie.' I pick up my rucksack and pull on my jacket, 'that's why they pay me the big money, and thank God that they do.'

I curse under my breath.

'See you when I get home. Love you.'

'Love you too.'

*

'Where will you be?'

'I'll be at the recharging station across from the burger place. You know, the one with the good looking girls wearing nothing but hot pants and tight tops. I'll be in a blue Chelsea hoodie and black trackies.'

'Discrete,' I grimace, 'and the package?'

'In my jacket. It's everything that you asked for.'

'No issues?' the guy's a crook, and in my experience all crooks are untrustworthy, even high-end ones.

'No. All on the money. You...' a moment's hesitation, 'you have the fee?'

I let out a long sigh, 'yeah, I have the extortionate fee that you and your boss are charging. Not exactly value for money. I hope it's all going to a good cause.'

He laughs, 'yeah, yeah. A good cause. Yeah. That's a good one.'

I'm a little too abrupt, 'don't be late Suko. I don't have time to waste.'

I feel his breath down the phone, 'I'm never late Brody. You'd better be on time too or the deals off.'

'Just be there and don't get followed. There's a lot riding on this.' I'm running out of patience with this guy.

'Oh yeah? I know the outline but not the details. You wanna elaborate?' I don't like questions.

'Let's just say that you'll have all the details you need come sun-up.'

'Sun-up? Who the hell says sun...'

I disconnect.

*

The night envelopes me like a comfort blanket. I walk down Lester Avenue. The pods are nose to tail, moving in unison to a slow beat. They're filled with people on their way to work; pale, dispassionate faces like zombies in boxes. The pods glisten with organic light emitting diode displays signalling their autonomy and soulless intentions. No-one needs a driving license in the twenty second century and everyone pod shares, times four. Just hop in with your co-workers and press go.

I walk. I hate the things. Too isolated. Too claustrophobic. I like the air on my face. I might not get the sunlight but I can sure as hell get the air. That's mine, that's a free man's prize and no-one will take that from me. Not tonight.

Tower blocks rise high into the night sky, their carcasses emblazoned head to toe with eye-melting luminance, moving advertisements for fizzy drinks, restaurants, TV shows and home improvement products. Through a sliver between the buildings and despite the immense light pollution I can just make out a few stars. They're there, I can see them. But they seem an eternity away.

This end of town is the dark end of the Split Twelve program. These lights aren't interrupting anyone's sleep. No-one is sleeping. The day/night has just begun. I feel bile rise in my mouth and I spit it out. It disgusts me.

I turn down the Meadows and pull up the collar on my jacket. It's cold but that suits me fine. I work better in the cold. I can see my icy breath in front of me and it provides me with crisp clarity. This can't continue. I won't let it. After tonight we will be free.

I can see the lights on in Jenna's front porch and I smile. My sunlight in all this gloom. She and the kids are my world, my engine, my crutch. I could not exist without them, could not put one foot in front of the other or open my eyes every night. As someone once said in one of those early, overly sentimental Hollywood films before everything went to rats and people stopped talking like that, she completes me. She does.

I approach the door and take a deep breath. She opens it before I have the chance to ring the bell. She is radiant.

'I thought it was you.' She smiles her beautiful, illuminating smile and we hug. I bury my face into the crook of her neck.

'I missed you baby.'

'I missed you too sweetie. How have you been holding up?' She takes my face in both her hands and looks deep into my eyes. I struggle to hold back the tears.

'It's been tough, keeping up the act you know? I feel like I have their eyes crawling all over my body all of the time.' I grab her waste, 'but I'm doing it baby. I've been doing it,' I tuck a lock of hair behind her ear, 'for us.'

She pulls me close, 'I know, I know. And me and the kids, we are so lucky to have you. When will it be done?'

I kiss her soft lips, 'tonight. It will be done tonight.'

'Are you sure baby? Christian keeps asking me. He's very demanding, on my case all of the time, I…' she looks agitated but gathers herself, 'it's just that, this should have been done weeks ago…'

I grab both of her hands. 'It will be done. Tonight. I promise you.'

She smiles, happy, 'I can tell him?'

'Tell him to be ready.'

*

It took me three years to get the security clearance but I finally got in. It had meant a little innovation on my part but desperate times called for desperate measures.

Jenna was reluctant at first but eventually she could see the bigger picture. It wasn't as if we were breaking up. We just needed the inside track. And sleeping with the daughter of one of the bosses was a pretty fast track to approval.

Caitlyn was the other end of town. The light end of Split Twelve. The privileged end. But I made contact. Social media at first, then a crossover time rendezvous in an uptown wine bar. Crossover time only lasts for an hour so it took an awful lot of rendezvous to get past first base. But I could tell that she was into me. She was excited by the deception, the intrigue, the princess and the pauper love story. She spoke well, I spoke very poorly. She knew a bisque from a soup, champagne from a bottle of fizz and a fillet mignon from a pork chop. I'd grown up poor from working class parents, living in an old terraced estate before they re-housed people and knocked them all down. She had grown up the wealthy daughter of an executive senior Vice President of Omega

Power, the largest power conglomerate in Europe with a share price that made shareholders extremely happy and investors extremely rich. When she introduced me to her father he went nuclear, if you'll forgive the pun, but even he knew that he couldn't stop her from seeing me. Her mother liked me from day one but I was no fool. That was because she hated her ex-husband. Her dad gave me a job, at the lower end of the pay spectrum and still in the night shift, but I was in. Caitlyn agreed to Split Twelve nights, moving from her Finance Director daytime position to a managerial role, and we got a place together. To seal the deal I proposed and daddy reluctantly allowed it to happen. We had a fantastic wedding with all of the bells and whistles, hundreds of guests, horses, a string quartet, a world class soprano, a cake as large as our apartment and a cost five times greater than my yearly salary. And all the time I was keeping contact with Jenna and my babies. And Christian, my friend. They were patient and understanding. We all were.

'Hey Brody. How's it going?' Ray snaps me sharply out of my day-dream with a hard slap on the back. He's a sixty year old technician with a beer belly and thinning, greasy hair.

'Evening Raymond,' I put my rucksack in my locker, close the door and turn to face him, 'any news?'

'Nope. Reactor's just ticking along as usual. We had a pump shut down during the day shift but maintenance got it back up and running in no time. That's about all the excitement I can give ya'.' He pats me on the shoulder, 'how's that cutie of yours. Still letting you touch her ass?'

I laugh, 'Yeah, I still get it three times a week if that's what you're asking.'

He gurns at me, 'you are one jammy son of a bitch you know that? Don't know how you did it but you need to share your lil' secret with ole Ray. I haven't swung my leg over anything since Barbara died, and that was fifteen years ago,' he holds up his gnarly hands, 'I'm getting blisters Brody, blisters!'

I laugh hard and wave him away, 'sorry Ray, can't help you. She's not into old geezers,' I cross the hall to the shop floor, 'but I can put in a good word for you with her nanna. She's eighty but I'm sure she's just as keen as a little girl in a sweet shop.'

'Yeah, yeah. You kill me Brody. Just you wait until you're my age. Just you wait!'

The screens on the shop floor are ablaze with data. Sometimes I have to put on my sunglasses just to avoid the headaches. It's about the only use these old sunnies get nowadays. Ever since Split Twelve began, some twelve years ago. I take a reading from the magnetic field generator. All is good. All ninety nine and a half million people in the United Kingdom will be getting their power rations today, all thanks to Omega, the corporation with a heart. Except half of them will get it during the night. When they should be sleeping.

I pour myself a strong black coffee. I need the caffeine hit. The coffee is hot and bitter, just like my mood. I look around me. All it takes is one malicious software code to bring this whole illusion down around our heads. One code that has the dexterity and finesse to outsmart the many hundreds of firewalls that protect the master control firmware from cyber-attack and nasty intentions as bad as Ray's jokes. One code that can shut down the protective magnetic field and over-ride the complex cooling system, causing the power plant to go into hibernation. One of the benefits of fusion power. No emitted radiation, no mass casualties. Just chaos. Blissful chaos. An event designed to wake the zombified population from their slumber, to re-ignite the passion and the desire in people, to galvanise the masses to fight those in charge and take back their sunlight.

They said it was due to overpopulation. The planet had become too full (nine billion and counting) and space exploration had hit the buffers. Too expensive and not practical. The Mars expeditions that were supposed to kick start the space program had failed. No natural resources, no practical way of creating a sustainable and habitable environment and no government with the necessary funds or desire to make it work. Earth was it. Period. And there was no room. Not when everyone hit the streets at exactly the same time every single day of every single week of every single year. This, they said, was the best way to ease the congestion issue, help reduce crime, free up the streets and generally improve our quality of life. That was the propaganda and most of the population bought into its hypocrisy.

Except we knew. Christian and I. We knew. There was room, there was plenty of room. You see, fusion power takes up resources from the sea. Sea water is a great source of lithium and lithium is an essential ingredient for a fusion reactor. One of *the* essential ingredients. And with fusion power plants now the globes only source of sustainable and reliable power the world needs a lot of lithium. The reclamation of sea water from the Mediterranean and the Black Sea, now enclosed due to the Gibraltar dam project, has meant that those sea levels have fallen substantially. And over the many, many years that corporations like Omega have been harvesting lithium there have been huge growths in useable, habitable coastline as well as additional small islands, popping up regularly like zits on a pubescent teenager. Two or three every five or so years. Places with the space and the resources to house thousands, millions. Except those places are restricted for the selected few. Those that know they are there and those that control the power. People like Caitlyn's family. People I had grown to loathe.

*

It's lunchtime and I'm at the rendezvous.

Suko hands me the device wrapped in a paper towel. Christ, he looks shady. This is supposed to be an invisible transaction. The only thing less invisible is the glaring sign overhead, declaring 'the best little asses delivering you the best steak sandwiches in town.' I glare at him.

'Is it what we agreed?'

'It's exactly what we agreed. We got the Worm to write it.' The Worm is the underworld's equivalent of typhoid. Any code that he writes is like a pandemic to a corporate computer system. It gets in, it wreaks havoc and it's virtually incurable. Devastation.

I smile, 'that's good, that's really good.' I pull back the towel and flick on the light. It looks like its operational but it's difficult to tell. Highly secure computer code is now delivered by laser beams. Algorithms are contained within complex arrangements of colours, levels of luminance and direction of light, injecting instructions directly into the brains of a computer. It's a sign of corporate paranoia, the rich and the powerful no longer willing to run the risk of some cyber urchin creaking open the door of a networked firewall. Everything at Omega is strictly off line. The beams themselves can be delivered from meters, even miles away, as long as the operator has visual access to the central core.

'You got the dough?' Suko shifts his gaze along the street. We're in a dark corner of a side alley but the road is heavy with traffic. It always is.

'Yeah, I got it,' I tap my pocket, 'Christian raised it with help from the Syndicate. There's a lot of people counting on this thing working,' I look down at the package in my hands with limitless hope.

Suko chuckles, 'well you can tell that cyber freak that he's chosen wisely. No-one can do the work that the

Worm does, and the Worm can't do what he does without authorisation from the Bishop.' He sighs, 'and you'd better not forget what you promised him.'

I look up, 'the Bishop?'

'Yeah, the Bishop.'

'What we promised the Bishop? What, aside from the three and a half million euros in my pocket?'

'You know full well what I mean,' he's agitated.

'Well go on then,' I throw my hands up, 'enlighten me.' I'm astounded. 'What did we allegedly promise, on top of the frankly extortionate fee charged for what probably amounted to three days of work, tapping at a computer in a dimly lit apartment whilst drinking copious amounts of strong, black coffee?'

Suko laughs, 'what did you promise? You don't remember?' He looks around, exasperated, like he has an audience, 'you don't remember? I can't believe this…he don't remember.' He slaps his head and looks me in the eyes with a glare that suggests he wants to cut my throat using a blunt tin can. The laughter drains from his voice. 'You promised him a place in that chopper and you'd better not forget it kid.'

I swallow my saliva. This must have been Christian. It most definitely wasn't me. 'But there's only six seats on the helicopter Suko. We can't have.....we can't have promised that.' There's desperation in my voice. The seats are all taken; four for me (Jenna and I, plus the kids) and two for Christian and his partner, Selma. Everything else is going to be handled later, when we've settled, when the chaos has abated and the Syndicate has taken control of things. This was going to be our reward for carrying out their instructions, for the years of sacrifice, for the endless nights where Jenna had lain awake crying, knowing that I was in the arms of another woman.

'Well,' he flicks my forehead, 'Brody,' he grabs my shoulders, 'my boy. You'd all better just shuffle up a bit,' he laughs a hoarse, cruel laugh, 'after all, he's a big bloke is the Bishop.'

I hand over the money, but I'm deeply troubled. We, Christian and I, are going to have to figure this out. This is unworkable. We may have to resort to drastic measures. That helicopter will just about hold the six of us. Any more and it's not getting off the ground and it certainly won't make it across the Channel.

Suko takes the money, gives me a goodbye smirk and disappears. The transaction is done. The rest is up to me.

*

'You're late Brody,' Ray is at his workstation, manipulating messages from the central system, ensuring the power is being distributed correctly across the internal network. I slide the package into the top drawer of my pedestal.

'Yeah, sorry Ray,' I flip open my laptop, 'bloody nightmare at the sandwich stall,' I slide my eye over the scanner and wait for the screen to come to life, 'ran out of bread. Can you believe it, a sandwich shop with no bread,' I ape a laugh, 'It's like a pub with no peanuts, right?'

Ray looks at me with curiosity, like he's trying to crack a code in my subconscious. His unblinking eyes look me up and down as if he's just found that I've been on the take. Then, all of a sudden, he bursts into laughter, 'a pub without peanuts….a pub without peanuts….that's good Brody! I'll have to remember that one,' he slaps his hands on the desk, his face red, spittle frothing on his chin.

I breathe out and gaze at my screen. Everything on my dashboard is running as normal. All is quiet on the

Omega front. At least for now. I need to call Caitlyn. I let the computer sync and walk into the kitchen with my earpiece in.

'Hey baby. How's your day,' her voice is welcoming and as smooth as single malt.

'Oh,' I sound deliberately downtrodden, 'I've had better. We've had a magnetic flux in one of the reactors drop dangerously close to minimum and the maintenance guys are scratching their heads. I'm going to have to hang back to re-set the system once this all gets sorted,' I sigh as if my whole world has fallen through a large chasm in the floor, 'I guess I won't be back for dinner. Can you apologise to the Braehmer's for me darling?'

'Oh sweetheart, that sounds just awful. It always happens when we have plans,' I hate lying to her but it's a necessary evil under the circumstances.

'I know, I know,' I pause for effect, 'you know, if it gets sorted quicker I'll get home for dessert but please don't get your hopes up,' and for added measure, 'I know I won't.'

'Okay honey. Well, just stay safe.' She sounds genuinely concerned.

'I will baby. Thanks for understanding,' and now in for the kill, 'Hey, baby?'

'Yes darling?'

'I know this is an imposition, and totally out of process, but....well, it's just that Farrell's on holiday and I need to get this damn thing sorted today.' I'm trying to be as innocently ignorant as possible.

'Okay, what is it?' She sounds suspicious but I figure that might just be my paranoia kicking in.

'Well, it's just that...well, to give the guys access to the magnetic source I need to open up the reactor housing. To do that I need to be able to over-ride the central...'

'Core.'

'That's it.' She's got it.

'And to do that you need one of the corporate key codes...' Her tone is flat and unyielding.

'You've got it sweetheart.'

'…which I'm not allowed to give you.'

I take a big intake of breath. 'I know and,' I breathe out, 'and I wouldn't be asking you if your dad,' the devil, 'wasn't away in the Caribbean with Deborah,' she hates Deborah, 'having the holiday of a lifetime.' I smile to myself. This is a good play.

Silence on the other end of the line. Complete and utter silence for three or four seconds. Too long for me to be comfortable. 'I don't know darling. This is…'

'Unreasonable, I know honey.'

'It's beyond unreasonable. It's a downright act of gross misconduct. Even daddy couldn't save me if the board caught a whiff of it.'

I wince, 'I know, I know. But how unhappy will they be when half of East Sussex goes without power this weekend.' I wait for an answer to no avail. 'And they've got no way of knowing sweetie. They'll have no reason to even suspect anything. It'll be just another day running just another power station in just another town in just another country.' Still no answer. I'm beginning to wonder if she's still on the other end of the line. 'Your dad and your step mum can enjoy their holiday in complete relaxati…'

'83zHH49?!'

'You'll have to…' I scrabble around for a pen.

'I said 83zHH49?!' I just about catch it, 'and she…is…*not*…my step mum!'

*

I feel bad for Ray, I really do. He's a good bloke, with a good heart and a nice family. He even supports the right team. But he's an obstacle and the stakes are way too high for me to be sentimental. The only sentiments I can afford to have are for Jenna and the kids.

He's not even looking when I take the largest adjustable spanner I can find and club him round the back of the head. All I get from him is a low grunt and the sound of someone crushing a water melon. There's blood, more than I expected but not enough to make me feel ill, and I think he pees himself. I haven't got enough time to dwell on it. The next shift starts in forty five minutes.

I open the access panel in the wall and slide out the console. I pull out the scrap of paper from my pocket and type in the key code. After two attempts I get it right; my forehead is dripping with sweat and my hands are shaking like an alcoholic with a bad case of the DTs.

Once I press send I hear a low hum and the panels nearest to the reactor slide back to reveal the core; effectively the brains of the whole system. It radiates like a polished emerald in the morning sun, thousands of light pulses firing in multiple directions in hundreds of controlled sequences, setting off commands that surge around the building, instructing and managing safety systems that keep under control the enormous amount of power being generated in such a small space envelope. If you could take the sun, put it between your hands and squeeze tightly so that you condensed it's unfathomable and terrifying energy into a tiny pea then you would have the basic principle of the fusion reactor.

I reach into my pocket and pull out the device. I hear a groan from behind me. I spin round.

Ray's eyes are open, blood is trickling from his mouth.

'What the hell are you...' his words trail off as his eyes open and close rapidly.

'Shut up Ray. You don't understand.' I get back to business.

'What the hell...' he's trying to sit upright but failing miserably.

'Leave me alone Ray! This is nothing to do with you!' I glare at him as if he is an annoying puppy tugging at the leg of my jeans.

'You'll destroy the...'

'Reactor. I know.'

'Yes but...' he's dragging himself along the floor, a slug trail of blood on the concrete behind him.

'Yes but, yes but!' I turn to face him, 'just leave me alone will you!'

'Our families! No power. No heat....' He's face is a mass of red blood vessels. He's going to give himself a coronary at this rate. Frankly he's beginning to irritate me.

'I get it Ray, but I know what I'm doing. This is for the best,' I believe it, 'for everyone.'

Suddenly he's upon me with his box cutter. He shoves it into my thigh like he's slicing a cooked chicken.

'AAAAARGGGHHH!' The pain roars through my body like a hot skillet on cool skin. He claws at my face but my size and my youth are in my favour. I grab the knife, bite his fingers until he lets go, and plunge the bloody blade into his retina. I push it in deep as his body thrashes and convulses and I watch, blood oozing from my leg wound, as he slides away from me onto the polished floor like a slow raft into the open ocean. I've killed him, I know that. But I can feel no remorse.

I tear a strip from his overall and tie it around my leg like a tourniquet. It will stem the blood if not the pain.

I wash my hands in the kitchen and check my watch. I'm down to twenty minutes to get the job done and get away. I recall that the core is on a timer and if left unattended for more than a few minutes the panels will close and it will be inaccessible with the same code for twenty four hours. I have no time. I need to move.

I grab the device and approach the central field. I have one shot. My eyes are blurry from the pain. I grip the small rod in both hands, kneel down and take aim. The core is around eight metres away. I've practised with distances a lot greater but this is now the real deal. I have one shot and one shot only. If the beam misses then all of this will have been a waste. It will be over.

I cannot allow that.

*

'It's done Jen'. It's done,' I'm crying, 'grab the kids and get to the checkpoint.'

'Oh Brody, is it true?' I can hear the trepidation in her voice. As if she could have ever doubted me.

'It is, it's,' I wipe my cheek, 'it's over.'

The alarms blare behind me, the warning lights at the gates are spinning frantically and I can hear the sound of distant sirens. The whole place is in lockdown but I've planned ahead. I have an escape hatch in one of the gates and I was originally responsible for setting the exit codes. I walk out as if I'm leaving after any other day at the office. By the time they watch the video of me causing all of this anarchy I will be long gone. And, in any case, it will be of no use. The virus is incurable. This plant will no longer generate even a watt of power.

'Grab the bags and meet Christian at his place. He has the pod programmed,' I duck behind a tree as the drone police vehicle approaches, 'I've got to go,' I hear the low hum of the engine as it passes to my left, 'I...I can't wait to be with you.'

'Oh baby…' she stifles a sob, 'me too. And the kids. We'll be together soon.'

I disconnect and climb into my vehicle. It's a low flyer and can carry me as far as the meet. These modes of transport are designed for local travel, getting traffic off of the streets and into the air, helping to alleviate congestion in some of the more built up, inner city areas. They're quick and efficient but absolutely useless for long journeys. Fortunately I'm not going far. We had planned for that.

I activate the power and four small blades whir into life, lifting me seventy feet vertically upward. Within three or four seconds I'm being propelled forward at a speed of eighty miles per hour, the trees and rooftops whistling by like freshwater trout in a stream. I can see far enough into the distance to note some twenty or so police drones racing to the scene of the crime. They'll be fully armed and authorised to use lethal force and I feel much safer in the sky. Those things are not known for their pragmatism. Within thirty five minutes this whole area will be plunged into complete darkness. I wait for it to close in on me. The darkness is refreshing. It will be our protective blanket, our ticket to freedom.

*

Christian is here. Thank God. He approaches from behind the barn. I look back at the city from our hilltop vantage point. It's completely black. It amazes me how something that shone so brightly and for so long can be extinguished so suddenly with the simple flick of a metaphorical switch. The authorities will direct all of their resources at the unfixable power plant. No-one will be looking for us. I set down the craft and walk across the wide expanse of lawn.

'You made it.' Christian is tall, maybe six foot three and has long white hair. He was the victim of a violent trauma as a young adult and his hair colour, once a vibrant blonde, changed overnight. He wears a pale blue, cotton shirt and beige slacks like he's set for a day at the office.

I look down at my bloody hands and wounded leg, 'of course.' I look around me, 'where's the chopper?'

Christian smiles like a comforting father, 'it will be here soon.'

'And Jenna and the kids?' I can't wait to see them, I feel my heart bursting through my chest in anticipation.

He cocks his head at the barn, 'they're inside waiting for you.' He steps aside and lets me pass.

As I walk towards the barn, a low illumination emanating from what must be a lit stove inside, I notice Christian's car and one other. It looks like a BMW Falcon, a high end vehicle with a top speed of two-fifty, a battery that runs for two weeks straight and with a manual over-ride for out of city cruises. Either Christian has had a huge pay hike (unlikely in his line of work) of there's someone else here. I put my hand in my pocket and close my fingers around Ray's bloody knife. Just in case.

'Something bothering you bud?' Christian rests his hand on my shoulder. I jump, startled.

'What?' I turn and face him, 'no, no. It's…' I look up at him, his smiling eyes seeking to comfort me, 'it's been a long wait and a hard day. I just want this to be over.'

He pats me softly on the back, 'it will be my brother,' he ushers me forwards, 'very, very soon.'

I reach the rickety barn door and push inward. I'm startled.

They're all here. Jenna, my children, Samuel and Ella, Suko, Caitlyn and that evil crook the Bishop. Even the bloody Braehmers are here. Just sitting there around the stove, looking at me like I've just waltzed in from outer space. Caitlyn's crying. What's she crying for? How does she know these people? What has Jenna gotten herself mixed up in? Why has my best friend brought these people here?

'Baby, it's over,' Caitlyn doesn't know that this is a set up. She still thinks we're husband and wife. I look awkwardly at Jenna.

'I…I'm not sure what's going on, but,' I look at Christian like a child looking at his father for help, 'I need to tell you something Cait'.'

'No Stefan, *we* need to talk to *you*.' Caitlyn stands up and walks towards me.

I look at Jenna, my eyes are pleading at her, 'Jen? What's going on? Who's Stefan?'

'Listen to Caitlyn, Stefan. She will tell you everything you need to know.' Her arms are folded across her chest like she's trying to keep me out. The kids aren't even paying attention, they're both reading from their palmtops. I want to go over and hug them into me, tell them how much I love them and that I did all of this for them.

'Chris', I…' I turn my head but Christian stands behind me as if he's trying to block my only means of exit. What the hell is this?

'Baby, we love you. We all do,' Caitlyn holds her arms out as if presenting me to the audience. Jenna loves me. I know that she does. The kids love me too. But Suko? The Bishop, the big, fat thug of a man sitting in the corner like an over-sized, gelatinous oaf? He doesn't love me. Last time I met him he threatened to kill me. I hate the guy. Caitlyn points to them one by one, 'Sarah, little

Steven and Jessica, my brother, your father, our neighbours, James and Louise, your brother Christian.'

'My *what*?' I look at Christian, 'my brother? *My brother*? I don't have a brother…' I look at Christian but he's nodding, 'I'm an only child, my…' my tongue is dry, my hands are clammy, 'my parents abandoned me when I was a baby. Jen'…' I point at Jenna but then realise that Cait' called her Sarah, 'Jenna knows all of this, but you won't. I never told you because we were…' I correct myself, 'we *are* a lie. A big, complicated, terrible lie. Fabricated by Christian and I so that we could execute our…' I don't know whether I should be saying this in front of all these people but what the hell, 'execute our plan to shut down the power plants and escape the country. You see it was…' I feel on unsteady legs, 'it was brilliant. Cause utter chaos and mass confusion, use distraction as a weapon, create panic and uncertainty. You see the reactor, *this reactor*, is the sole source of power to the autonomous tracking beacons located all over the country, and without that power we can't be spotted, not for days, weeks even. Gives us enough time to get to...' I pause, 'well, to get to where we're going. We can escape as if invisible, under the blanket of darkness, this awful *darkness*, the very thing that they have imprisoned us in, *all of us*, for as long as I can remember.' I look from Caitlyn, who is crying, to Jenna who is sitting calmly, her legs crossed. 'Jenna, tell her it's...' I hold my hands out to her, 'tell her, *please*.'

'I can't Stefan because it's not true,' she stands up and walks over to me, 'and deep down you know that.' I hold my arms open for her and I'm shaking my head, tears trickling down my cheeks. I want so badly to hold her, to pull her to me and fall into her soft brown eyes, away from all these lies and crazy fantasies.

'Jen'....baby.' She walks past me and grabs a hold of Christian's hand, slipping an arm around his waist. 'What...'

'You know this Stefan, you know all about Sarah and me,' Christian kisses my wife, Jenna, on the top of her head, 'but since the accident you haven't been yourself. We are all here to try to help you. You and Caitlyn,' he looks up at Caitlyn who is standing directly in front of me, tears on her cheeks, her mascara sliding down her face like wet, black ash from a burnt out building, 'but you need to help yourself and try to remember.'

My mouth hangs open in disbelief. I don't know what to do or what to say. I'm mesmerised by the flickering light on the barn walls, interrupting the blackness enveloping us with impish fireflies of dancing radiance.

'Your treachery knowns no bounds Christian, I...' I'm boiling with growing rage, 'I always knew you were after her, but this?' I can feel the cold blade burning a hole in my pocket. My fingers slide around the handle and it feels good.

'And you,' I point at Caitlyn with my free hand, '*you* are part of this. You knew all along didn't you? Didn't you, you…' I take a step towards her and spit the word into her face, '*bitch*.'

She gasps. Suko comes up behind her and embraces her.

'Suko! Why are you even here?' I glare at him with all of the hatred in my heart.

'My names not Suko, Stefan. I'm Jules, Caitlyn's brother,' he holds Caitlyn tightly as she sobs into his shoulder, 'goddam it, you were the best man at my wedding.'

I can't believe the deceit being played out here, and the organisation that this must have taken, for them all to give me the same bloody lie and to tell it so convincingly. 'And if that's true *Jules*, who the hell is he?' I point to the big lump resting its big, bulging backside on a bale of hay in a shady corner of the barn. The Bishop.

'I'm your dad son,' he has a big, resounding voice that echoes around the cavernous barn, reverberating at me from all directions, 'maybe not much of one, but your father all the same.' He gets up and ambles over, standing next to Caitlyn and Jules in a terrible trio of dishonesty, treachery and deception.

I'm losing my voice, 'and the…' I glance at my children, both lost in their own little worlds, oblivious to the game being played around them, 'the kids?'

'They're our kids Stef',' Christian looks down at me almost apologetically, 'mine and Sarah's. They're your god-children and they love you very, *very* much.'

My heart is ripped from my chest and thrown into the abyss. They're not mine. We're not running away

together. I am not a father. I am not who I think I am.
I'm...*no-one?*

'You had an accident Stefan,' Caitlyn takes my
hands, 'a terrible accident at work. You were in hospital
for a very long time,' she touches my face, 'and when
you woke you didn't know who you were, who *we* were,
who...' she stifles a sob, 'who *I* was. You started to
believe this story that we were being held prisoner during
the night and that we were all oppressed in some way by
some imaginary authority. You mistrusted people,
everyone, couldn't stand to be around anyone. You didn't
know yourself, who you were and you created strange,
fictional characters for all of us. You hated the company,
probably because subconsciously you blamed them for
what had happened to you, and you started to believe that
you were married to Sarah, *Christian's Sarah,* and that
you and I were...' Jules, *Suko*, grips her round the
shoulders, 'a *lie*. You concocted a plan for some kind of
escape and we all went along with it. We were *told* to, by

133

the doctors. They said that with this kind of paranoiac amnesia correcting what you believed to be true could be disastrous,' she looks around her for support and some of the others nod their heads, 'don't you see Stefan? We hated it but we had to do it.' She grips me so hard that I can feel her nails digging into my forearms. The pain feels good, '*we had to.*'

'What about Ray?' I can smell his blood, can feel his life slipping out of him as I hold him in my bloody arms. I think of his family. What they will think of me? A life ruined and for what?

'I'm here Stefan.' Ray steps out of the shadows like the ghost of Christmas present. He has both of his eyes. He looks fine. As fit as a sixty year old fiddle. 'Right here. And don't worry. I've been keeping on top of everything for you while you've been…away. Ready for you when you come back.' He smiles and gives me a wink.

'But I…' I can't comprehend what I'm seeing. I draw the knife from my pocket and look down at it, expecting to see the blade caked in tissue and blood. But it's my key, my house key, and there is no blood. I look at my leg and there is no wound. Nothing. The pain has gone and my skin and trousers have knitted themselves back together like some kind of rapid self-healing miracle. My face is hot with shards of burning glass, my vision is swimming like I'm looking at the world through deep, murky water. I feel my legs turn to mush and then I hear the sound of my head hitting the soft hay from some far away, distant place. I'm crying but I don't know why and I think of my family. Then everything is black. Like the night. It engulfs me and there is no escape.

*

I awake and I'm in Christian's spare room. Caitlyn is sitting in a chair reading. Her face is firm, resolute. She is smoking a cigarette. She doesn't smoke.

135

I hear a sound from outside, a whirring of blades. A prolonged gust of strong wind shakes the curtains and rattles the windowpane. I can see through the leaded glass. There's a light in the darkness and it rises up into the night sky. I see six faces. Christian, Jenna, the children, Suko and the Bishop. The Bishop is laughing, his chins trembling like bloated jellyfish in the low tide. I watch as they wheel away and disappear into the distance, slowly fading into the black. They can only escape at night. Only by night.

Bed Bugs

First came the bed bugs. Tiny foot soldiers of a thousand strong parasitic cimex army marching in dreadful unison, blood red exoskeleton torsos clambering over the dystopian landscape of her cotton bed linen. All shapes and sizes, male and female, young and old; they were determined nymphs, both indestructible and ravenous. Emitters of powerful pheromones, they guided each other with invisible and soundless communications, drawing one another to their unwitting prey in stealthily silent night raids. They crawled up Becca's arms, in her ears, crept delicately over her closed eyelids and, worse still, slipped in between her partly opened lips and into the warm, breathy, moist cavern of her mouth. They made house in her pillow case, in the creases of her sheets and in the folds of her duvet. They found solace in her nightgown and fortitude in her underwear. They dined out on a feast of her dried skin and warm, life juice and fed their infants on crumbs of marmite toast and cheese and onion crisps littered like morsels of delicious haute cuisine in the thick pile of her carpet.

They expanded in numbers like rodents on caffeine, multiplying three and four fold daily. They hid during sunlight hours, leaving no trace of the destruction they had wreaked in the dark and cold of the night, only to spring back to life when the lights were out and Becca's head touched the scarce solace of her eiderdown. Even when they weren't there she sensed them, felt their many black, marble like eyes gazing at her from beneath the skirting or from under her dresser. She scratched incessantly.

Then came the flies. The god awful flies, buzzing in the dark like Messerschmitt 109s in a dog fight, attacking her face and neck like X Wing Fighters dive bombing the Death Star. Becca would flap and flail her arms as if in the middle of one her epileptic episodes and sit up with a start, brushing malevolent bluebottles away from the flat, oily landing zones of her forehead and cheeks. Once or twice she would feel their hard bodies slap against her palm as she thrashed around in the gloom, falsely and temporarily shrieking in victory, only to be plunged back into despair when the dazed and confused winged beasts regained consciousness and renewed their unyielding onslaught.

Flashback. Uncomfortable feelings of intense anger.

God, she needed to sleep.

Benjamin could help her. Benjamin would know what to do.

But Benjamin wasn't around.

Benjamin was an artist. A painter. A tortured soul with a beautiful mind and a unique talent with canvas, oil, colour and brush. Her room was awash with his radiant imagery and fluorescent, episodic epiphanies. He was a hidden gem, an untapped resource of artistic ingenuity and originality and, like all geniuses, from time to time he needed his own hidden space and solitude.

Becca had met Benjamin when they were at art school together. He was struggling to find his own artistic voice whereas she was prospering in interior design. They had exchanged glances in the coffee queue. She had bought a vanilla latte and he an americano, no sugar from the artisan coffee house where the waitress that she admired had worked until recently. The blonde girl with the red freckles. She and Benjamin had started up a random and colourful conversation and he had immediately struck her with his intensity and sense of benign hopelessness. She in turn had entranced him with her boundless energy, endless enthusiasm and tireless lust for living. They were opposites in the truest sense of the word and the attraction was inevitable.

She had been deeply embarrassed when she had had an episode on their first real date. They had been out at an Italian restaurant for the evening; he had had the antipasti and she the spaghetti carbonara. They had drunk some red wine and she had felt a little tipsy and on the walk home, after pausing to give the handsome homeless gentleman her last remnants of change, she had felt bold enough to stop to kiss him. Her heart had been pounding and her pulse racing and, moments later, she awoke in his arms, prone on the pavement and with no memory of her fainting. He had smiled down at her while she lay there, vulnerable like a small, abandoned puppy and his genuine and touching fear and concern stole her heart.

Flashback. Fuzzy and dizzy head.

They had moved in together almost instantly, deciding to relocate his things into her flat. His suitcases mainly contained easels, paint brushes, alcohol and some personal effects; clothes, bathroom items and such. Benjamin wasn't much of a hoarder.

Things had been good for the most part. Her parents didn't approve, believing him to be abrupt and ostentatious, but Becca saw through all of that and loved him for his intelligence, wit and creative brilliance. Sure, they had the occasional row, massive blow outs that usually ended in him throwing things in her general direction and punching fist sized holes in his canvas, but what young couple full of vivacious lust and raging hormones didn't? She infuriated him from time to time with her affection and sense of protection for her friends, some of which were of the opposite sex, and he in turn could frustrate her with his bipolar and explosive mood swings and general, chaotic untidiness.

But there was love. Deep love. He was her sociopathic soul mate and she his random and belligerent muse. And of course there was passion. Ravenous and unsated passion that consumed them like the mother of all plagues, draining them of all thoughts and desires other than the unstoppable need to hold each other (and others) in a sweaty and breathless embrace.

From time to time he would strike her, softly at first but then harder and more frequently. He said it turned him on. Mostly it turned her off.

Jonah didn't like Benjamin, but Jonah didn't like anybody (except for Lola. He *had* liked Lola). Jonah preferred his own company but he liked Becca, just a little too much to be comfortable around her when Benjamin was at home, but Becca didn't mind. She didn't see Jonah in that way and he knew it. He was her best friend and confidante, she the prized possession that was just out of his desperate grasp. Their relationship suited them both.

Jonah was a poet. He wrote about love, lust, life, death and loneliness. He typed with his left hand because he had lost his right arm in a boating accident when he was young, the barely grown limb ripped right out of the shoulder socket by a mooring rope that hadn't been unravelled correctly from the dock. It never phased him and the sense of loss simply added to the desperation in his prose.

'You got a lot of bugs.'

'I know right? I can't shift the bloody things.'

'You need to get a guy.'

'A guy?'

'Yeah, you know? A bug guy.'

'I can't afford it and, besides, when Ben gets home I'm sure he'll fix it.'

Jonah sniffed loudly, 'he couldn't fix a nosebleed, let alone a crustacean infestation.'

Becca smiled, 'yeah. You're probably right.'

'Where is he anyways? I haven't seen him around here in a while.'

'Oh,' Becca waved it off, 'we had a shout off,' she touched a hand to the dark, purple and yellow bruise under her shirt, 'and he left,' she glanced round the room nervously and then laughed, 'but he'll be back. It normally takes him a few days to cool down.'

'If you ask me he needs to take a month. Take a good look at himself. You know, he's not good for you, but I know you don't want to hear it and I'm just a jealous, lovesick guy and he's the love of your life and his art inspires you and blah, blah, blah…'

She threw a pillow at him, tiny invertebrates scattering like dust mites and landing randomly on her carpet and duvet. 'Jonah, you're so funny.'

The air felt thick and the room fell silent. Jonah looked down at his hand, turned it over and stared at his palm, 'you've got to sort it out Becca.'

'I will. I'll talk to him. When he gets back,' her cheeks were flushed, 'I'll sort it, I will. I'll make him see sense. When he gets....back'. She gazed at the black dress hanging on her wardrobe door.

Jonah looked up and peered at her through large, chocolate brown eyes full of longing and trepidation, 'I....I meant the bugs.'

She glanced down at her lap, smiled to herself and nodded, 'yeah, I get it.'

Flashback. Tears. Sobbing. Trauma.

Two more days passed and still there was no sign of Benjamin. His paintbrushes lay on the easel like discarded weapons, red paint dabs on canvas like bloody teardrops. She missed him and wondered after him, imagining him to be desperately alone and yearning for her like he might yearn for sustenance or nicotine. It would be dark in there, dark and soulless. Deep down she knew that he would come out only when *he* was good and ready and when the time was right. *Her* time was right. She missed him.

She was busy installing a UV lamp to kill the flies when her mother called to check on her.

'Is *he* there?'

Becca sensed the barely stifled disapproval, 'no Ben.....Ben's out?'

'Out as in outside or out as in gone?'

She dug her nails into her palm, 'as in *not in*, mother. As in he isn't in the building.'

There was a heavy sigh and a cold silence, 'well you know what I think but I won't waste any time in repeating myself.'

'No, please don't.'

'And what about you?'

'About me?'

'Yes, have you had any more,' there was a slurp as Becca's mother sipped what was most probably peppermint tea, 'any more instances?'

'Instances of what?'

'You know very well Rebecca. Any more *fits*.'

Becca had suffered with epilepsy all of her life but since puberty the fits had subsided and had developed into random blackouts or syncope, a condition where the blood pressure drops suddenly and intermittently, starving the brain of oxygen and glucose and causing the sufferer to collapse. All very normal and only dangerous if standing somewhere precarious when the moment occurs but consequently she couldn't drive. That didn't bother her because, as she always said, how could she miss something she had never had? Some memory loss was normal but usually recoverable. It gave her....cravings, but in the most part she could control them.

'No, not that I'm aware of. I got an infestation though,' she swiped an insistent fly away and crushed two bed bugs between her fingers, blood trickling down her palm and wrist.

'An infestation? Of what?'

'Insects, all over my room.'

'Oh dear, I have told you to stay on top of the cleaning. Those things are attracted to filth.'

'Mother!'

'Well....you take after your father. One swipe of a duster and you think the place is spotless. As I've said to you many times before,' Becca mouthed the infamous line, 'cleanliness keeps the soul pure.'

'Well then I guess I'm going straight to hell.'

Her mother muttered something under her breath and then asked, 'will we see you tonight?'

'Tonight?'

'At the gala. Don't tell me you've forgotten. Your father will be so disappointed.'

'Shit. The gala!' She smacked a palm on her forehead, inadvertently crushing one of the larger arthropods and smearing its broken shell and blood onto her brow.

'Rebecca!'

'Sorry mum, sorry…' she reached for a tissue and scrubbed feverishly at the goo and gloop, 'of course I'll be there. Er…eight o' clock right?'

'Seven dear. Dinner is at served at seven,' another heavy sigh, 'will *he* be coming?'

Flashback. Falling. Grabbing. Clutching.

Becca shook her head and blinked twice, 'no, no. I don't think so. He's...' she thought fast on her feet, 'he's working on a commission for the library so...' she looked at her mobile phone. No texts. No calls. *No sound.* 'He'll probably have to work through the night to get it finished.'

'Pity,' her mother could barely hide her delight, 'will you be coming alone?'

Hardly, Becca thought to herself. She couldn't bare to spend the whole evening by herself amongst her parent's snobby friends. 'Jonah!' she paused for breath, 'no, Jonah will be coming with me. You remember him? The poet?'

'Ah yes,' there was an amused chuckle, 'the chap with one arm. Poor fellow.'

Becca smiled through a grimace, 'yes that's him. The very talented poet who happens to have a disability. You really have a *wonderful* turn of phrase mother.'

'So people tell me. Don't forget, dress code is evening gowns and dinner suits. Don't let us down dear.'

'Perish the thought.'

'Okay, that's done then. See you at the King Charles Hotel at seven sharp. Don't be late.'

And with that she hung up. There was a fizz and a pop and the UV lamp claimed its first victim. Becca shook her head and laughed. Jonah was going to kill her.

Flashback. Breaking noises. Pain in her hand and shoulder.

Jonah arrived at six-thirty, dressed in an oversized, black tuxedo, white shirt and dicky bow, one empty arm hanging loose and flaccid. His jet black hair was greased to one side.

'Well?' he smiled a juvenile yet maniacal grin, 'how do I look?'

Becca smiled lovingly back, 'like a superhero.' She kissed him on the cheek and ushered him in.

'This place smells funny.'

'It's the fly lamp. It's claimed the lives of a dozen or so already.'

Jonah took a closer look, 'sweet. I love these things.'

'Don't touch it though. You wouldn't want to injure your good hand.'

'Funny. I wasn't going to touch it. Just wanted to take a look at the Kentucky fried insectoids. Ooh. Gross,' he picked up a large housefly and waved it around, 'you got this one good. Medium rare or well done m'lady?'

Flashback. Blood. Lots of blood.

'You're disgusting. Don't play with your food.'

Jonah pretended to eat the fly and licked his lips. 'Delicious.'

153

Becca was in her dressing gown, her hair tied back in a bun and her make-up delicately applied, 'I've just got to throw on my dress and shoes and then we're good to go.' She grabbed her dress from the wardrobe and ran her hand down the door, glancing anxiously back at Jonah.

'Well, don't be shy. I won't look.'

She slapped him on the shoulder, 'I don't think so buddy. I'll be in the bathroom.' She looked back and winked at him as he struggled to prevent the blood from rushing to his cheeks.

Jonah sat down on the small couch and looked around the room. Small but homely. Nicer than his place but it hummed like an abattoir. He picked up a magazine, some celebrity rag, and thumbed through a few pages. Pictures of wannabes and their latest significant others, all people he didn't care about, all people who were dragging out nothing careers to rack up as much cash as humanly possible before their names and faces were retired to the cobwebbed annals of the museum of 'no-one gives a shit.' He threw the magazine back onto the sideboard.

Another fly hit the lamp. He licked his palm and ran a hand through his hair, checking his face in the mirror as he did do. He didn't look too bad. Not bad at all. If that gimp really didn't come back maybe he would stand a chance, he thought to himself. Just maybe. He waved his hand in front of his ever so slightly crooked nose. Too bad her apartment smelt so bad.

Becca's phone was on her dresser and it was unlocked. Jonah couldn't resist and he picked it up. Text messages from friends and family, some from him. None from Benjamin since last Saturday lunchtime.

Baby, I really love you but you really have to get new friends.

Baby, where have you been. I've been home for two hours and I have no idea where you are. Who are you with?

Becca, honey, I want you to myself. All to myself. Does that make me bad?

Maybe it's time baby. I can't wait any longer.

That freak Jonah is an imbecile. Can't you see he is using you? Let's just phase him out like the others.

Jonah's blood was boiling. As if Becca would ever agree to that. As if she would ever let that idiot come between them. He'd been around, what, five minutes and he thought he could drive a dagger into their friendship! Did he really think he could do that? What gave him the right to even try?

Jonah tossed the phone back onto the dresser but his aim was off and it tumbled onto the floor with a clunk and a clatter.

Suddenly there was a noise, a song. It sounded like…like the theme tune from Doctor Who. The sample played over and over repeatedly, the piercing theremin soundtrack cutting through the air waves like shards of shattered crystal. Jonah looked down at Becca's phone and there was a picture of Benjamin glaring up at him, taunting him. Jonah must have accidentally hit dial when he had tossed it aside. But that meant....

Jonah jumped up from the sofa and grabbed Becca's phone, bashing the red 'end call' icon repeatedly. Only the ringing didn't end and Jonah reluctantly came to the realisation that his careless act of launching the phone onto the floor had caused the software to glitch, freezing the phone in 'call' mode. He couldn't even turn the phone off. The screen just blinked mockingly, Benjamin's smug face grinning up at him like he knew exactly what was going on and was loving every second of it. Jonah clawed at the edge of the phone for the battery compartment but to no avail. No battery access. He carefully placed it back on Becca's dresser and searched frantically for the missing phone. That idiot Benjamin must have left without it. He guessed that there must have been some kind of altercation, but then that didn't really surprise him. They were always at it, the pair of them. Odd though, he thought to himself. Odd that he hadn't come back to collect it.

Ooh wee ooooooh, weeeeeeeee ooooooooooooooh

The song played over and over incessantly like a child repeatedly calling for its mother. Jesus, he cursed under his breath, hasn't this guy heard of voicemail?

He searched under the sofa, behind the dresser, in the wardrobe and behind the curtains but the phone was nowhere to be seen. The sound seemed to be emanating from the bed but Jonah really didn't want to look.......there. The whole duvet was riddled with those disgusting creatures. He was astounded that Becca actually still had it in her room, let alone slept in it.

He gently peeled back the sheets and the volume grew louder. He put his hand to his mouth. There were little spatters of blood where Becca must have rolled onto the bugs during her sleep, crushing their little armadillo-like torsos under her naked back and buttocks. It looked like someone had loaded a paintball gun with the little critters and let loose all over the divan. Dead bug bodies lay scattered and lifeless like they were in the aftermath of some terrible battle.

The phone kept ringing as the tune melded with the low humming vibration of the call receipt alert; a sub-woofer undercurrent that gave him the ice cold willies. He wanted it to stop *so bad*. He didn't want Becca to come out of the bathroom, pick up her phone and ask him why he had been snooping around in her messages.

He glimpsed a handle tucked between her duvet and the foot of Becca's bed and realised that she had one of those flip top beds, the ones where the bed folds upwards on hinges and gas struts, providing access to a large storage space underneath. That's it, he thought, the phone's under the duvet! All he had to do was flip the bed, avoid contracting plague and pestilence from General Crusty and his creepy crawly friends, grab the phone and turn it off.

He reached down, grabbed the Velcro handle tightly and pulled.

Suddenly the bathroom door opened and there was a simultaneous creak and a thud from behind him. He looked up and saw Becca in the doorway, her hair tied back with fluorescent scrunchies in shabby pigtails. She was wearing a stained yellow nightdress and brown, threadbare slippers, her eyes rolled back in her head like glassy white, slightly rippled, marbles. She was smiling a lopsided, spittly smile and she was holding a rusty pair of nail scissors in her right hand while her left hand waved at him, her crooked fingers opening and closing one at a time as if she was manipulating the air holes of an imaginary flute. He felt a grip on his shoulder and he turned and saw Benjamin, wide eyed and excited, as if he had just found the world's most exciting piece of art, the wardrobe behind him gaping open, the doors jutting outwards like the mandibles of a terrible praying mantis. Jonah suddenly wondered whether he had he been in there all along?

'Hi Jonah. Didn't expect me to be here did you? You know, I really didn't appreciate what you were saying about me,' Benjamin nodded across to Becca, 'she's having an episode old boy. It's not looking good for you.' He winked at Jonah as if they were sharing a scandalous secret.

Ooooooh eeeeeeh ooooh, Weeeeeeeeeeee ooooooooooooh.

'What? I…I don't understand?' Jonah was struggling to comprehend what was going on. That bloody song was befuddling him. What was Becca doing? She looked more than a little crazy.

'When she gets like this my old mate there's really not a lot I can do,' Benjamin laughed, 'I try to talk her down but there really is no stopping her,' he laughed, 'I mean, *she's wild!*'

Becca was shuffling towards him, her eyelids fluttering incessantly and her pigtails flapping up and down like the wings of a mortally wounded bird.

'Becca, Becca! It's me,' he implored, 'Jonah!'

'Unfortunate but necessary. If she doesn't get her kicks once in a while then she really is unbearable. Didn't you realise that? I mean you're supposed to be her best friend...' Benjamin smiled with more than a faint hint of smug amusement.

Jonah didn't understand. He opened his mouth to speak but no words came out.

'You only have to look at what she did to them...'

'What, who?'

'The ones who came before'

'The ones who came before what?'

Benjamin let go of his shoulder and pointed a long, bony finger into Jonah's chest.

'Before *you*.'

Jonah looked down at the yawing chasm of the bed and put his one remaining hand to his mouth. Three pairs of black, gelatinous eyeballs looked up at him from the sockets of waxy, decomposing faces, their arms and legs bent at crooked, unnatural angles while bugs and slowly creeping magnolia coloured maggots, spongy and tender like half-cooked rice pudding, slithered their way into mouths, ears, nostrils and other assorted orifices.

Jonah saw the surprise in the face of his ex-girlfriend, Lola, the shock in the gaping mouth of the young freckly girl that used to serve them coffee and eggs in the café on the corner, the silent cry of the homeless man that would joyfully sell them their Big Issue every month with the toothless smile of a happy, hopeless soul.

'*What the hell is going…?*'

'What did you think had happened to these poor chums my friend? Just vanished off the face of the earth like nothing had happened? *Didn't you even care?*' Benjamin grabbed Jonah firmly by the shoulders. 'You must have realised that she was a little odd. Let's face it, her room is a downright disaster zone. Didn't you notice the *smell*? *And the goddam bugs?*'

Becca lunged towards Jonah with the scissors and they nicked his cheek just under the right eye. He cried out and thrashed his upper torso, trying to shake off Benjamin's grip but the artist was way too strong.

'It's okay my darling,' Benjamin looked across at the seemingly maniacal Becca and smiled grimly, 'he's a bit feisty but he'll hold still just a little longer, won't you Jonah?'

Jonah kicked out and struck Benjamin in the soft sacks between his legs. There was a crunch and a loud exhale as Benjamin released his grip and fell to the floor in a crumpled heap. Jonah cried out in triumph just as Becca raised her arms, both hands gripping the scissors as if they were a medieval scabbard, and plunged the jagged blades into his bulging jugular vein. Her eyes came back into focus, she uttered a distant and longing 'Jonah', shuddered from her toes, up through her legs, into her long, slim torso and out to the tips of her fingers and fell, limply to the floor.

Jonah grabbed his severed vein, trying to keep the blood from spurting from his weakening body, but he tripped and fell backwards into the dark space, falling and flailing hopelessly. He landed softly between Lola and the homeless man and they smiled as if to reassure him. Lola's cold, fetid cheek rested silently on his forehead and he remembered when her cheek wasn't so cold. The homeless man's arm fell across him as if he was imploring Jonah to take his last Big Issue, 'just one more my friend, for old time's sake.' The coffee girl's one remaining eyeball stared at him through the black, her mouth upturned in a ghostly, half-smile. He recalled her caramel latte and almond croissant and wished he had been a better tipper.

The bug army, previously busy taking turns at nibbling on coffee girl's cheeks and tongue and homeless man's arms and chest looked up in unison, changed direction and marched towards him, making ground faster than he would have thought possible for those with such miniscule limbs. They reached him swiftly and decisively and crawled up his neck and arms, slipped under his shirt and up his trouser legs, rappelled through his hair and clambered over his eyes, into his ears and onto his mouth. The quickest and fittest got to the gaping wound first and dived into the warm stream of liquid squelching through his fingers, his one hand proving useless as a tourniquet. He knew he was slipping away and quietly bid farewell to

Becca. Whatever she had become, whatever she had been, he still loved her. A tear rolled down his check as tens of thousands of legs lightly caressed his skin as the light grew dim and the mouth of the bed closed. He was entombed in its hellish carcass as his many friends welcomed him.

TimeBomb

Mud and noise. Repetitive rattling like tiny ball bearings being shaken in a tin can. Deep, humming bass, like the subwoofer of the best digital, Dolby surround sound on steroids. Light and dark, acrid smoke stinging nostrils and burning the eyes. Ears ringing, hands trembling, tears flowing.

A man, late forties in a grey tracksuit. He is kneeling, his hands are over his ears, his pupils are dilated, his sense of direction numbed, disorientated, discombobulated. He is confused.

'Football….biscuit…..48965322…..incomplete… ….incomplete'

He is pushed to the ground, he swallows a mouthful of muddy earth and chunks of grass and stone.

He wrestles in vain with his assailants but they are gone. He pushes himself up on his elbows, and peruses the front of his tracksuit. Mud and blood is smeared from his neck to his stomach. He spits out wet soil.

'Football....biscuit.....48965322.....incomplete...
.'

A crash, a fizz overhead, shouting. He can hear pain but he feels none. He sees a face but when he blinks it evaporates. Either side of him it is dark but he senses terror and.... anticipation. He looks at the gold signet ring on his left hand. It is soiled with earth but he can see his own face reflected in its golden sheen. He looks older and wiser than when he last saw himself, carefully wet shaving in the bathroom mirror just....that morning. Yes, that was it. He is shaking uncontrollably.

'Football....'

A yell and something falling. Grunting and heaving. Something flies past his ear like a bee or a mosquito. It is quick. He attempts to brush it away.

'Biscuit….'

A brilliant white light and then utter dark. He places his hand to the ground to steady himself but something tears his palm. He yelps.

'48965322….'

Something striking an object, like a hammer hitting a cabbage. Crunching and squelching. Screams of pain. They are deafening and he puts his bloody hands to his ears to block out the sound. He feels a hot needle strike his shoulder and he is shoved backwards by an unseen force. Loud booms, mud striking his face and body, an arm hits him on the forehead. He rolls onto his back and looks at the dark sky above.

'Incomplete….'

*

A shiny, cold surface, his back is moulded into the metallic material like memory foam but it is smooth like aluminium. His hands are held in soft clasps, he is naked and he is relaxed. He hasn't felt this peaceful since….well since he was at home, back at the ranch with his mother and sister. That was so long ago. He can barely remember the details of his bedroom, the wide open spaces and the workshop where he built things.

There are pulsing lights, no windows. A song that he cannot place. A melody that is warming to him, like the lilting call of a nightingale. It seems to emanate from all around him. He looks from left to right for Gloria but she isn't there. When did he last see her?

There are shapes ahead of him, moving and interacting. At first he thinks they are animals, apes even, but they are holding things, moving things, placing things. He is suddenly afraid that he has done it again.

Fallen off the wagon, had way too much to drink whilst out with his old college buddies, winding up in one his old haunts, the 'Society Rooms' or 'The Rodeo'. He can't afford for that to happen, *won't* let that happen again and so he pulls on the clasps round his ankles and wrists. They dig into his flesh like razor wire and he screams.

There is more movement, shapes leave the chamber and return with other shapes. He blinks to clear the fluid from his eyes. His vision is blurred and his eyes are streaming. He shakes his head once, twice. His neck and jaw ache.

'Where am I?' he shouts at the shapes. The shapes stop moving and turn to him. 'What is going on here? This is false imprisonment people! This won't turn out well for you when I get out of here. And I *will* get out of here!'

Mumbling and giggling. Three sharp strobe slights blind him. He turns his head away and squints his eyes. He grunts from the pain in his head. He licks his lips to moisten them. His mouth is so dry. Is he hungover?

'I suggest this stops right now! You've had your fun. I get it, I'd gotten myself into a bit of a mess and you thought you'd play a prank on me. Well now the jokes over and you can let me go. It's funny, really,' he curls his lips in a snarl, 'but if I'm not out of here in the next two minutes *I swear to god* you will all end up in jail for a *very long time!*'

A blurred face fills his vision.

'Do you remember?'

*

He's up early as usual. He kisses his wife Gloria on the cheek, her dark hair enveloping her regularly and repeatedly moisturised and tightened face like a shroud. He brushes his teeth and shaves. He looks good, far too good for his age and better than he could have expected at this stage of his life and with everything that has happened to him in the past year. *What a rollercoaster.* 2022 had been *the best* year. He still had to pinch himself to prove that it had really happened. Jeez. A boy from a ranch in Ohio and look at him now. *'I did good mama.'*

He smooths back his red hair, throws on his grey tracksuit and heads downstairs to the gymnasium. Thirty minutes on the treadmill and then he will be fit and ready for the day.

He catches a glimpse of the TV as he walks into the studio which is surrounded by large, beautifully polished glass walls. The adaptive lighting comes on and the expensive, top of the range Track Elite machines are already running. On the big, curved LED screen he sees the latest news on CNN. The Koreans, at it again with their aggressive rhetoric and dramatic shows of military power. Military power? They had no idea.

He puts in his ear-phones, switches on his Spotify and sets the machine to four miles an hour, slowly increasing to eight. He sings along to the tunes; Sinatra, Cash, Diamond. He even slips in a bit of Jay-Z, particularly when the machine accelerates to top speed and he pushes it to nine.

Sweat forms on his forehead, on his back and chest and under his arms but he is focussed, driven and determined. Always has been. That focus and drive got him there in the first place and he'd be damned if anyone was going to prevent him from ploughing ahead like the cast-iron juggernaut that he was. That his mother made him.

He thinks of Gloria, how she stuck by him through all the bad times, when he lost himself with no direction or purpose. When he hurled into a tailspin. He thinks of all the girls that he had been with behind her back and he is ashamed. He'd been tempted since but he'd kept his little fella in his pants and, whilst there were no guarantees in his business, he fully intended to *try his best* to keep it that way. He thinks of the drink and the drugs, paying for gratuitous sex, getting into ugly bar fights and begging his uncle to get him out of trouble. All that is behind him now. Has to be. For the sake of his job and for the sake of his country.

He checks his pulse. One twenty. Not bad. Not bad at all for a middle aged man with a penchant for pastries, fried chicken and bourbon. He knows that today is going to be a good day.

He doesn't see the throng of people behind him, doesn't notice the headlines jumping from the TV screen like an action movie title sequence and doesn't hear the commotion and fuss and the doors to the gymnasium almost swinging off their hinges.

He just feels the gentle tap.

*

The face has a hand and it is prodding him. Touching his skin, his chest, his arms, running long fingers through his neatly trimmed, red curls. There are other hands and they are attaching things. Sticking things on him. Attaching things to his fingertips and toes, clipping things to his earlobes.

He shakes his head but large firm objects are placed either side of his temples to prevent him from moving. There is silence apart from the singing nightingale and the rustle of jostling and movement. He speaks but his words start to slur. 'My God,' he thinks to himself, 'I'm still drunk'.

'I....I don't know what you are....doing....but thish ish a very....very bad move on....on your part,' something pierces the skin just above his nipple and he winces, 'there will be....peoples looksing for me and....and they *will* find me.'

He sees the eyes and the mouth of someone who is obviously very curious. He or she appears to be very determined to complete the task at hand. He is starting to get more than a little afraid.

'I can pays you. Whatever you want. Names your prish....price and itsh yours,' he tries to make out a location, a scent, an object. Something to give him a clue as to who is putting him through this bizarre ordeal. 'I....I need to pee. You need to lets me go to the....the toilet. I will shoil myshelf man! *Have a goddam heart!*'

There is suddenly a bright beam of purple light from above. It is shining directly onto his upturned face. It doesn't hurt his eyes but it is warm and he can feel his skin begin to prickle. The remaining moisture in his mouth evaporates and his throat turns to coarse sandpaper.

'I....I need a drink,' he corrects himself, 'I need water.' His voice is cracked and hoarse. 'Are you listening to me? *I need a drink....water*!'

'*Do you remember?*'

'What?' he tries to make out the intonation and dialect, 'Do I what?'

'*Do you remember?*'

'Remember what? Do I remember what?' he doesn't understand and the voice is unfamiliar, unusual, 'Look, look...wait,' he speaks as calmly and as lucidly as he can, 'wait. You need to help me out here, I....I don't know what you mean. I'm sure that we can work something out but I don't know what you mean.'

There is silence and the shapes have withdrawn. It is just him alone, just him and the purple light illuminating his greying and deeply lined features.

'Hello? *Hello there*?' his head is fixed but his eyes flit back and forth, 'I don't understand. Do I remember what?'

A low hum. A shuddering. The room seems to swoon from side to side and back and forth repeatedly and incessantly. He feels sick to his stomach.

'Do I remember what?'

He belches and his head throbs. He can feel his heart pounding from behind his eyes and his palms sweating profusely. Fear encases him like an iron lung.

'Do I remember what?'

'Everything.'

*

He sits alone in his office; the huge, opulent space that wears the momentous echoes of the past as ornately and effortlessly as its rosewood chairs and olive green shag pile rugs. His tracksuit is still moist from the run.

Gloria had been with him but she was no help. Her usually heavily sun-kissed face had turned white with fear and she had been wringing her hands together as if trying to drain them of all bodily fluid. She had paced back and forth, back and forth, back and forth and had caused so much kinetic mayhem that he had asked her to leave. She had looked at him in shock and bewilderment but had begged him desperately, pleaded with him to make the right choice. For the kids.

He has no time. No time at all. No time to think, to consider, to map out the course ahead. It is as digital as that. Do it or don't do it. Either way there could be no going back from his decision, no second chance and no possibility of redemption.

The tablet volume is on mute but it is screaming at him in dreadful, calamitous silence. The house is full of people but not one of them can rescue him. He flips the card between his fingers as the leather bag lay at his feet, jaws open like a ravenous beast about to devour them all. It had been delivered to him as he had stepped off of the running machine, the studio gymnasium full of men in suits of all colours, creeds and causes. His aide had emerged from the throng like a bad omen, solemnly carrying the black briefcase, distastefully referred to as the nuclear football, and handed it to him. He had taken a step back and raised his hand to his mouth. *What?* Disoriented and befuddled he had asked for a moment. For some time where there was no time. He had wanted to pause his life right there and then, like the way Superman could do it. But he was no superhero.

He looks at the live stream on the LED screen, at the headlines, at the images. He looks at the authentication card – the biscuit. He memorises the OP PLAN 8010 attack code numbers. He curses under his breath as the door opens.

'It's time.'

*

Everything is a blur. Time fizzes around him in tepid slow motion, like a tornado on sleeping pills.

He sees the Secretary of Defence whose mouth moves in bullet time, speaking those dreaded words that demand his immediate authentication. He looks down at the biscuit in his hand, eyes it like a credit card with the worst rate of interest in history, and turns and walks to the large bay window. Those bloody Koreans. They wouldn't back down. All the diplomacy at his disposal and they throw it back at him like a used tissue. God damn it. *God damn.*

The attack codes whir round his head like the bullets from an AK-47, bouncing off the inside of his skull like ballistic missiles. He is shaking his head. He has no choice. They must act first.

The Oval Office is thrown into shadow. Something overhead. He looks out the window across the

White House lawn as the Secretary places a hand on his shoulder. There is a shape out there. An object above them. Dark and so very smooth. A loud humming; a stillness and sense of calm. He breathes in deeply and his chest is heavy and painful. He feels a strong vacuous pull like he is being sucked out of the window by a powerful and invisible force.

There is a whoosh and a pop and then….

Nothing.

*

'*We cannot allow it.*'

'Cannot allow what?'

He has been removed from the bed, or whatever godawful thing it was that he had been gripped within, and seated in a tall chair. He is clothed in his tracksuit and sneakers again. His hair has been brushed.

There are three shapes standing before him; the tallest one is in the middle with two shorter shapes, people even, either side. His vision is still impaired but he can make out basic forms; arms, legs, heads. He cannot make out the sex, age or colour. Simply that they are there.

'We cannot allow it.'

'Look, I need to get back to my family, to my job. There is a….' he can't quite remember but he recalls the emotion and the fear, '….a crisis. I am needed.'

There is a whirring above and he looks up. There are stars, millions of them. He can see them as clearly as he could see them back home at the ranch with no light pollution, no yellow hue to soften the clarity of the brilliant spots of light spattered across the night sky like white flecks of paint on a black canvas. He can see purple and green nebula, orange and white stars of different colours and sizes, planets of many flavours and varieties with clouds of gas and liquid combinations, too many to recall or mention. The space is vast and endless and he is in awe.

'What is this? Where am I?' He speaks as if dazzled by the imagery.

Something prods him and an energy leaps through his limbs like a snake springing to attack from its tight coil. He sees it. The black case being handed to him reluctantly by his young and ambitious aide.

The football.

He starts to cry, 'I didn't do it, *I didn't!*'

Another prod and a bolt of lightning shoots from the tips of his toes to the top of his skull. His cranium is on fire and his eyes feel like burning sink holes. He sees the card, rolling through his fingers like a poker chip.

The biscuit.

'*You must learn.*'

'You must understand me. I didn't do it. I was going to....yes. But I didn't want to. I...' he pulls his head away as if he is about to be struck by an almighty force, 'I had no choice!'

A comet flies by as the third shard of electricity makes his teeth clamp together, almost shearing the tip of his tongue. His eyes roll backwards and he recounts the memorised numbers.

'48965322....'

Tears are pouring down his face as he sees his children, Toby and Jeremy, running down the stairs at Christmas, excited to see what Santa has brought them and whether Rudolph has eaten the carrot from the saucer they have left on the front stoop. In his mind's eye they are suddenly engulfed in a blaze so bright that their flesh is peeled from their bones, their hair singed to tiny black wires, their frames reduced to smouldering embers. He yells in pain.

'It was incomplete. I didn't do it,' he cries long sobs of despair and remorse, 'I didn't do it….it was incomplete,' his voice reduces to a whisper as the floor beneath his feet evaporates. He watches as the entire universe, in all its wondrous and majestic glory, opens up before him. His tears fall like emerald droplets and turn to ice as they are swept away in the desolate vacuum of space, 'it was….*incomplete.*'

A grey face, long black fatherly eyes, thin, pursed lips, a black tongue, tiny holes for nostrils, leathery skin, spindly arms with ribs and chest cavity exposed. He cries out. A long finger with black nails points at him accusingly. He is being judged.

'You must learn.'

A whoosh, a pop and then….

Nothing.

*

'Come on man!'

He looks up from his prone position on the ground. He sees the face of an armed soldier, no more than twenty years of age. He speaks with a British accent.

'Thank God. Thank God! You're here to rescue me. I have had such an awful time,' he sits up and brushes himself down, 'I need to get back to the House and swiftly. There is no time to waste my boy.'

'I'm sure you do but we need to get you to safety first, sir'

Strong arms and hands grip him and he is dragged backwards. He feels elated. He has no idea how he has gotten here but he is so happy that he is out of….that place. Has it been a dream, a nightmare even brought on by some kind of intense pressure or traumatic stress? God knows he has had enough of that over the last twelve months, longer even. He quietly vows to take his physician up on his offer of a holiday in his apartment on the quiet island of Mauritius. Who knows, he might even invite the wife and kids.

People run past him shouting and screaming and there is noise, loud noise. He is being hauled backwards like a ragdoll but he yields to the force, welcoming the feeling of evacuation and freedom. Those idiots who had kidnapped him were now feeling the full force of the coalition army, and lord knows they deserved it. He is the President for Christ's sake. The President of the glorious union that is the United States of America. Talk about going for the money shot.

One of the soldiers holding him up grunts and falls to the ground, as does another to his side. He looks left and right and can see barbed wire and sludge. There are shapes, bodies, tens of them, all lying at crooked angles with blood and mud and human faeces caked on their fetid torsos. He looks ahead and sees flashes of light and hears tumultuous blazes of gun and cannon fire. He sees mines exploding, artillery catapulting across the void, human beings driving blades into other human beings, fathers and brothers being executed by each other, the hollers of fear, anger and futile desperation.

Finally he is yanked hard and he tumbles backwards into a ditch. A trench. Deep and wet and full of vermin and dead and injured young men. An officer bends over him, 'are you okay mate? Yankee is it? Didn't know you boys had made it out here yet, but we're sure glad to have ya'. We need all the manpower we can get,' he chuckles and points at the President's attire, 'don't go much on your uniform though.' The officer reaches down and places a muddy hand just right of the President's neck, 'did you know you've been shot....in the shoulder there?' He smiles an empty, inane smile, 'don't worry though. We'll have you patched up and back in action in no time.' The officer reaches up and pulls a silver box out of his jacket, 'do you need a fag mate? Or a swig of brandy?'

'Where....where am I?' He is shaking because he feels he knows the answer, no matter how impossible.

('*You must learn.*')

The officer rubs mud from his face and looks down at him inquisitively, 'where mate?'

'Yes, where....and....*when* am I?'

The officer laughs. 'Well if you don't know that mate you really are in a pickle.'

'*Just answer me man!*'

The officer takes his rolled up cigarette out from between his cracked and bloodied lips and looks around in quiet desperation. His eyes portray the empty gaze of a lost soul trying to find his way home. A man-boy left to fend off the greedy, vindictive hands of Satan himself with no more than a rifle and a bayonet.

'Why, you're on the front line, mate.'

The President places a trembling hand to his mouth.

'The fields of the Somme in northern France.'

He gasps in sickening terror and steadies himself on the upright of a wooden ladder.

'It's the year of our lord nineteen hundred and sixteen and, God willing....' The officer places his hand on his heart, his cigarette smouldering between his fingers like the fuse of a great bomb, *a time bomb*, about to detonate and send them all to futile oblivion, 'the last days of this Great War.'

Up above he sees a shape, a vehicle that is dark and so very smooth, racing through the night sky like a speeding train heading towards a long dark tunnel. With a flash and sonic boom it is gone. Mortar shells explode at the top of the trench and the officer urges him to take cover. He sits down in the wet and the mud and the blood and he holds his hands out in front of him. Hands that could have done so much good but ultimately had failed him. He sees his mother and she is beckoning to him, calling him back home to the ranch. He sees the first lady and his children and hopes that one day he will see them again without the cloud of a nuclear holocaust hanging over them. He knows he has much to prove. Prove to both himself and to those things…those *beings*, human or otherwise, that snatched him from the jaws of his own terrible defeat before he could commit the most ungodly of acts. They had deposited him back….here, *specifically here*, for one reason only. So he could learn.

He lies down as the muddy water laps over him and he laughs. A long, hoarse and tragically prophetic laugh that echoes through the endless tunnels of time and space.

Mister Trick

Fufu sat in the back of his van and removed the sticky and sugary boiled sweet from his mouth, clasping it between his forefinger and thumb like a treasured, priceless jewel and raising it to his good eye for inspection. He smiled serenely and held it up to the van's internal light, its radiance dimly illuminating the interior of his transit, the soft glow eradiating the orange sheen of the confectionary delight, its warm sunrise gently kissing his hollow cheeks and pitted forehead. He smiled, raised the top hat balanced in the palm of his other hand and placed the sweet in the vacant slot left by an errant Liquiorice Allsort that had been displaced by wandering hands the day prior. The sweet made a soft schlurp as its sugary glue made contact with the purple crushed velvet encapsulating his Jaxon and James. He licked his fingers and wiped them on his polka dot, silk handkerchief.

He gazed at the photograph propped between his brown, leather suitcase and his trolley full of tricks, treats, cardboard effigies, furry and bouncy balls, colourful rope, party balloons; long, short, thin and fat, loud and squeaky horns of various sizes and assorted gadgetry and trinkets of revelry. The picture reminded him of another time.

'One, two, three, four five...' He sang as he sat his hat down to dry while running a silver comb through his slick hair.

'Once I caught a fish alive...' His voice was thin, childlike and full of good cheer. He held up his suit jacket and inspected it for hair and debris.

'Six, seven, eight, nine, ten...' He plucked a stray hair from his nose and wiped his sticky handkerchief across his sweaty brow.

'Then I let him go again...' He held his boots up, spat on them, a long phlegmy spit that hung lazily from his lip and wiped his shirt sleeve across the surface, smearing the spit and gloop but wiping away the mud and dust from the leather and stitching.

'Why did you let him go...?' He stopped, caught his breath and laughed.

'Good question....' he gazed at his sullen expression in his hand-held, silver mirror and frowned. The blue tattoo of the bulbous tear that rested permanently and irrevocably on his left cheek twitched as he blinked both his good eye and the glass one. He pinched the bridge of his nose between his forefinger and thumb and grimaced.

There was a noise outside as a car raced past, the van rocking violently from side to side and almost causing him to drop his looking glass. He thanked his lucky stars.

'What do you think Ro Dro?'

He turned the mirror around and looked at the reverse side, his image on that mirrored surface was three times as large as the other side, as if he were looking at himself through a telescopic lens. He could see the acne scars on his cheeks, the shaving marks on his chin and the bloodshot and mottled veins in his one good eye. He pooched his plump lips.

'Beats me my Fu Fu, beats me....'

*

'Well, where is he Drew?'

'How the hell should I know?'

'He should have been here thirty minutes ago,' Lydia was animated and stressed, a toxic combination that was threatening to overflow with vitriol and bile. She was frantically fighting to keep her famously volatile temper in check. 'If this is another of your cheap-skate attempts at saving money then you're going to be in deep trouble,' she hissed at him, 'and I *mean* it.'

'Look,' Drew Hermann downed the dregs of his lager and placed his pint glass on the table. He looked over at his sister-in-law for solace but she was shaking her head knowingly, 'I know Rufus, Lyd',' he placed his hands on her shoulders and smiled, 'he won't let us down. The poor sad sack hasn't got it in him,' he laughed reassuringly.

Two boys and a girl, no more than five years old, ran around them both, each trying to tag the other. The boy with the brown hair slipped and fell over, scraping his elbow on the maroon carpet, and the blond boy and the girl with the red curls ran off screaming across the dance floor.

'I'll get bofe of you two! Don't you wuwwy!'

'He'd better not let us down Drew,' Lydia, her sweaty dark hair sticking to her scalp and in her eyes, glared up at him from her five foot nothing 'punch your lights out' frame. 'You'd really better hope he's going to show,' she grabbed one of the children by their arms, '*and soon*.' She strode off in the direction of the toilet and spoke to the young girl with a thinly veiled irritation, 'come on Maisy, you're going to pee yourself.'

Drew turned to Lydia's sister Tara and her husband Eli, a tall, long haired fellow and shrugged.

'You're a bloody prat Andrew,' Tara was scowling at him, 'it's just like you to try to save a buck by booking the weird bloke that cleans the windows at the shop. He'd better not screw this up.'

Drew dug his right hand in his pocket, rummaged around and pulled out a tenner, 'Tara, he's half the price of most of the kids entertainers round here. Most of them want three hundred quid. He's doing it for one-fifty' he smoothed the ten pound note out in his left palm, 'and anyhow, he owes me one.'

Tara took a step towards him and grabbed his arm, 'you're a typical Hermann, always looking to cut the cost by whatever means,' she looked down and smiled at Tabitha in her pram, 'we've been planning this for such a long time. Do you really want to spoil this little one's big day?' Tabitha cooed up at her, spit bubbles forming on her lips and her big brown eyes screaming out for a hug.

'I won't,' Drew leaned over to the bar, 'and *he* won't,' he smiled back at her, 'I promise.'

Tara looked back at Eli and shook her head. 'Well if you're saving so much money you can get me one,' she plucked the ten pound note from his fingers, 'Debbie, mine's a pink gin and tonic,' Drew reached for the money but she whisked it out of his reach, 'with ice.'

Shawn Darling, a stocky, barrel chested, wild boar of a man with a salt and pepper goatee, buzz cut hair and forearms that looked like they were hewn from stone, stood next to his wife, Sandra, at the other side of the hall and scowled. He idly rubbed his overtly large hand across the pink and mottled skin graft that stretched from just under his chin, along the side of his granite neck and onto his robust shoulder.

'I don't know what she sees in him Sandy, I really don't.'

Sandra Darling plucked a hair from his shirt and smiled, 'oh come on now Shawn dear,' she glanced across the hall to the table next to the busy bar, Drew chatting to his sister-in-law Tara and a fraught Lydia yelling at the children to calm down, 'he's not all that bad. Maybe a little wanton and surely as disorganised as they come,' she sipped her red wine, 'but he's harmless.'

'He was a loser at school and I don't see much that's changed about him since then. Why the hell did she go and get herself pregnant with that bloke's useless seed.' Shawn's forehead was red, his cheek's flushed and he gripped his pint glass with hands that looked like they could crush it into sand with minimal effort.

Sandra glanced at her nails; long, dark red and professionally manicured, 'well Tabitha's a beautiful angel and if that's what Lydia had to do to earn herself such a lovely daughter then so be it. You'll just have to get used to the idea.'

Shawn grunted. 'I used to bash his head when we were kids and I could do the same to him right now. Little snot nosed oik,' he grimaced, 'his brother nearly bloody killed me and yet Lydia somehow decides that he's the love of her life. It's like she doesn't even remember.' He sighed ruefully.

Just then, with a whoosh and a pop, the double doors at the entranceway to the function hall swung open and in walked a man with little presence, a dour, musty odour and more than a whiff of pity, self-loathing and isolation. He was carrying a brown leather case and pushing a rickety, squeaking trolley full of seemingly old junk. His slick, white hair was swept to one side in a parting and his thin, black pencil moustache was stuck to his upper lip like it had been drawn on with permanent marker. His tweed jacket hung loose and threadbare and his beige trousers were baggy and a little too long. His brown shoes were scuffed and scratched and his laces were untied and dragging underneath his feet as if they were clawing at the floor for some sort of purchase. His plump belly sagged over his belt like a lazy, one-eyed walrus and his short, stocky frame was slightly stooped and withered.

'Where the hell have you been Rufe'?' Drew bounded over the floor in large strides and grabbed the arm holding the case, 'are you trying to get me killed?'

The newcomer licked his palm and wiped it across his hair, 'I'm so very sorry Andrew,' his voice was deep and subtle, 'I found myself otherwise.....engaged.'

'Engaged? Enga....well you're here now so let's get you set up,' Drew turned and looked back at the throng of guests, all sipping on their drinks, eating the expensive buffet that he had reluctantly forked out for and tapping their feet to the annoyingly repetitive pop music playing through the hall's tinny stereo system, 'the kids are going bloody ballistic.'

Rufus set down his case and shrugged. 'You...sure you want to go through with this Drew. Is this really what you and Tara....'

'*Lydia*'

'Lydia. Yes. That's it,' Rufus smiled, recalling, 'Lydia Darling.' He reached up and stroked a finger slowly across his right eye.

'Lydia *Hermann* now Rufus.'

Rufus Trowbridge smoothed down his side parting once more and nodded. 'Of course Andrew. I didn't forget.' He looked around him, 'how could I?' The adults were chatting and laughing, the children were running around and sliding across the dance floor on their knees, the babies were cooing and chuckling in their prams and carry chairs, the bar staff were pouring pints of lager and glasses of wine, the large, rickety function hall table was full of assorted finger food and a large, white cake with brilliant white icing and precise, pink writing. The small, shallow stage lay before them with four multi-coloured disco lights whirring and spinning. 'I mean it, you didn't have to give me this gig and we don't have to do it,' he nodded earnestly, 'even now.'

Drew looked at him in bewilderment and grabbed him by the shoulders, 'Rufus, look.' Drew checked himself and released him, 'I mean, Rufus….old chum. If you don't go through with this I'm afraid I'm for the high jump,' he picked up Rufus' tattered case and started to drag his trolley across the maroon carpet, 'I mean, I could get murdered to death,' he beckoned Rufus to follow him, 'I don't want that, not at all. And if you really are my friend,' he poked a finger at the beleaguered little man and smirked, 'any sort of friend at all then we have absolutely no time to waste.'

Rufus hummed under his breath, shook his head stoically and, like a reluctant child, trailed behind Drew as he manoeuvred his way through the crowds of children and various related and unrelated guests whilst always edging towards the side door. He flashed a knowing smile at Lydia (Hermann *nee* Darling) who was cradling Tabitha in her arms and entered the yawning room beyond.

*

Muriel Darling had had one too many pino grigios and yet, it appeared, she was the only one on her table who was oblivious to the fact.

'I mean, *hic*, Ruth, this is all a bit poncy don't you think,' she waved her pudgy arm around her, 'I mean, all this, *hic*, palaver for a baby who's far too, *hic*, young to appreciate it.'

Ruth Walters laughed, 'Oh, I don't know Muriel,' she took a bite out of a prawn vole-u-vent and winked, 'I'm enjoying the grub. I mean, I don't get out much now you know. Not after,' she brushed crumbs from her blouse, 'my Albert passed.'

Muriel downed the remains of her white wine and waved Lydia to get her another, 'oh don't be so, *hic*, morbid Ruth. That was seven bloody years ago,' she peered at her table mate over her spectacles, 'will you just get over it already.' She swallowed a handful of cheese and onion crisps and looked around her. 'I don't even, *hic*, know half of these bloody people and the half that I do know I don't much, *hic*, like.'

One of the teenage boys walked over and kissed Muriel on the cheek. 'How are you auntie? I haven't seen you since Bobby and Alice's wedding,' he smiled down at her affectionately, 'how are you keeping?'

Muriel put her glass on the table, pulled her spectacles down to the tip of her nose and leered up at the young boy with the tall, slightly too skinny frame.

'I'm sorry my dear, but...,' she punctuated her words with dour breath that smelt of white wine tinged with cheese and pineapple, 'who...the...bloody...hell, *hic*...are...you?'

'There you go mum,' Lydia reached over, Tabitha tucked under her arm like a delicate parcel and placed a large glass next to her mother. 'Just take it easy, okay. I don't want you swearing at Drew's family again. They've only just stopped talking about it and I could do without any more bad publicity after....' she turned to the young boy with the dark, foppish hair, 'oh, hi Michael. How are you?'

Michael looked from Lydia, to Muriel, to Tabitha, who was happily sucking on a chunk of soft, white bread and back to Lydia again. 'Fine thanks Lydia. Just popped over to talk to Auntie Muriel, but…'

'Oh for god's sake son. I was only, *hic*, joking…' Muriel took a large swig of her wine.

'Oh…oh, I didn't realise, I….' Michael's face reddened.

'You're Duncan's boy.'

'That's right auntie.'

'Duncan Weatherford.'

'Yep, that's my dad.'

'Duncan Weatherford, the bloody crook who charged me fifty quid to service my boiler.'

'Well, I…'

'I tell you Ruthie, *hic*, he came round, drank my tea, ate my biscuits, robbed me blind and had the cheek to smile as he left.' She picked up the glass and took a long sip, '*and* my hot water's still on the bloody, *hic*, blink.'

Just then, as if to spare young Michael from any more familial torture, the door to the right hand side of the busy bar opened and in walked a man with brown, calf-length, suede boots, green, pleated trousers with a cowboy style belt ordained with a silver, bulls head buckle, a custard yellow dress-shirt with flared sleeves, a red, velvet waistcoat with purple, love heart shaped buttons, white, silk gloves and a purple top hat upon which were placed tens of sweets of various varieties, flavours and sugary delight.

A fan-fare sounded over a stereo which sat to the side of the main stage, through which an anonymous man announced the oddly dressed character's bizarre entrance.

'Lady's and gentlemen, boys and girls, dogs, cats, tropical fish, antelopes, orangutans and whatever and whomever else is attending this glorious and salubrious event,' the audience, made up of nans, granddads, aunties, uncles, cousins, second cousins, third cousins, the elderly, the middle aged and the young and infantile all sat up, stopped talking and listened. 'May I welcome to the stage your host for this evening.'

The gentleman in the colourful garb struck a pose, his right leg cocked to one side, one arm held out to his left, the other tucked under his chin and his face tilted up to the ceiling.

'The one,' a smile.

'The only,' a wink.

'The oft imitated but never bettered,' a lick of the lips.

'The scourge of the seven seas, the master of deception and devilry, the man that puts the miss into mystery,' a two-step shuffle and a clap of the hands.

'Miiiiiiiiiiister Triiiiiiiick!'

The fanfare reached a tumultuous crescendo with a boom, bang and a cymbal crash and a few of the more receptive guests clapped and hollered.

'Well, hello there my children,' Mister Trick bent down, cupped his hands around his mouth and whispered, 'shall we begin the fun?'

With that he leapt up, skipped across the dance floor, did an almost perfect, if slightly rotund, cartwheel and landed feet first, with a spin and a shuffle, in the centre of the stage. He held out his hands for applause but only a low murmur emanated from the crowd.

The children, many of them under the age of ten, looked on in and wonder and awe but they were reluctant to leave their parent's sides.

Drew, his head bowed and his shoulders hunched, pushed the trolley across the dancefloor, its wheels squeaking eerily in the silence, and placed it by the side of the stage. He was grinning sheepishly and looking over at his hesitant wife through his brown, foppy curls.

'Well thank you my handsome assistant,' the colourful entertainer's voice was high pitched and wheezy, 'it's good to see so many smiling children in the audience this evening. We are going to have some real fun.' Mister Trick, his face adorned with a tear tattoo just beneath his left eye, his lips painted red with lipstick, his cheeks dusted with rouge and glittery stars drawn on his forehead, gazed longingly at the variety of guests. He had thick, drawn on black eyeliner around his eyes and when he blinked his eye lids were painted with silver glitter.

'And mums and dads, I think you're going to have some fun too.'

Auntie Muriel grunted into her wine.

Mister Trick reached to his left and Drew handed him a plank of wood which he had retrieved from his trolley, out of which hung three pieces of rope; one green, one yellow and one blue.

'Now come closer children, come now,' the children gradually and tentatively left their parent's sides, 'that's it, come to the dance floor and sit down so that you can see.' Young boys and girls, including the brown haired boy, the blond haired boy and the girl with the red curls, shuffled along the scuffed and battered wooden floor and sat down in front of the low stage. 'Closer, closer still. I need you where I can see you.' He chuckled, did a hop and a skip and exclaimed, 'I need a volunteer!'

The children sat in bashful silence and the parents began to whisper amongst themselves. Mister Trick looked at the children one by one, then up at the parents and then across at Drew by the side of the stage. He turned to Lydia who was fidgeting at the back of the hall. He could see that she was becoming irksome and he smiled.

'Well,' he muttered to himself, 'this won't do. It won't do at all.'

A few of the kids started to squirm on their bottoms.

'I can see that I'm going to have to pick a helper. Let's see,' he peered down at the young, expectant faces. 'Itsy, bitsy, teeny, weeny, yellow, polka, dot,' he pointed to the middle of the dancefloor at a young boy with spiky, brown hair, '*panini*. It's you my friend, come to the stage.'

The boy wiped his nose with the back of his hand, stood up, shot a glance at his parents and climbed over the children to the front of the stage.

'That's it, that's it, all the way up here,' Mister Trick looked at the boy and then up at the other children, 'and what's your name young man?'

The boy scratched his head, picked at his nose and exclaimed in a booming voice that was far too deep and resonant for his tiny frame, 'my name is Harry!'

'Harry, Harry,' Mister Trick ruffled his hair, 'well, ladies and gentlemen, boys and girls, let's hear it for Harry!'

The boy's parents whooped, the father standing up with his iphone pointed expectantly at the stage, and a few other relatives and friends in the crowd applauded.

'Go on Harry!',

'Get up there Hazza!',

'Give us a smile Haz!'

'Well Harry,' Mister Trick stooped down and held out the plank with the rope, 'what colour would you say that piece of rope is?'

Harry looked at the rope, held it up, looked at his dad and stated proudly, 'the rope is green.'

Mister Trick peered into the camera phone, his sparkling eyelids glittering in the spotlights, 'green you say?'

Harry smiled, looked at the children in the front row and confirmed, 'yup. It's green.'

'Well, young Harold,' Mister Trick turned the plank around to show him the knot of the rope on the other side, 'why don't you pull the green rope through the plank and see what happens.' Mister Trick looked at the crowd of children, their mouths open and their heads tilted to one side and winked.

Harry reached up, his pudgy fingers clasped around the knot, and gave it a big pull, the rope squeaking as he pulled it gently through the splintered plank. As he did so the rope changed from an olive green to a sparkly purple. Harry looked on in bewilderment, Mister Trick's face beamed, Drew tittered under his breath in glee, the children cooed and Auntie Muriel uttered an, 'oh for goodness sake.'

'Let's give Harry a huge round of applause!'

The children all cheered and Harry turned towards them and cheekily bowed, his right arm hand tucked across his tummy and his left hand held out in front of him.

'And before you go Harry, let me give you a little something.'

Harry turned and looked up at him.

'Do you like swords Harry?'

The boy nodded in confirmation.

Mister Trick reached into his trolley, pulled out a silvery long balloon and a shorter red balloon, pulled them twice and lifted them in turn to his lips. As he blew he pulled the end of each balloon and the floppy, latex material filled with air, creating one long and one short sausage shape. With a few flicks of the wrist and the twiddling of some fingers Mister Trick had tied both ends, twisted the red balloon around the base of the silver balloon and created a red handled, silver bladed cutlass.

'There you go Harry, now you're an esteemed pirate captain of the high seas.'

The children stood up and cheered as Harry took his balloon and swung it from side to side in a mock battle.

Drew clapped loudly, did a two-step shuffle and peered up at Lydia.

'See?' he mouthed at her.

'See what?'

Drew sauntered over and gave her a wink, 'I told you he would be good.'

Lydia wiped Tabitha's mouth with her bib and half cynically smiled at him. 'I don't know Drew, isn't he a bit...?'

He gave her a knowing smirk, 'a bit what?'

Lydia looked up at the stage, shook her head and said, 'a bit creepy.'

Drew supped on his lager and half-nodded, 'yeah, a little but he's...' he pointed at the stage, 'he's entertaining the kids. Even your cousin Edgar's boy seems to like him.' He pointed at the usually disruptive and rather spiteful Tegan who was laughing hysterically and pointing at the funny man in a 'sweetie hat'.

Lydia looked back at the stage, 'I dunno. He was weird at school and...' she looked around the room, 'I mean look at him. What does he look like?'

'He looks like a children's entertainer Lyd'. Tara...' Lydia's sister looked up, 'Tell Lydia. Tell her that this is what kid's entertainers are supposed to look like.'

Tara looked back at her husband and then across at her brother-in-law, 'I...I guess so.'

Drew laughed, 'odd as he is, at least he's keeping the kids occupied. Now all of us adults can take a breather from chasing after them,' he pointed at the children scattered around the floor of the hall, all entranced and amazed by the amateur magic show, and wiped froth from his upper lip, 'now I'd better get back to the prop department before the whole thing goes belly up.'

Across the hall Lydia's best friend Chloe was watching Mister Trick as he pranced across the stage, grabbing props handed to him by a captivated Drew as he pulled fake rabbits out of seemingly empty sacks, blew giant bubbles from a love heart shaped ring, made table tennis balls disappear underneath colourful paper cups and pulled chocolate coins from behind the wet ears of the little boys and girls.

She laughed with her boyfriend Danny who was finding the whole thing somewhat ridiculous.

'Jesus, this guy has more cheese than a french fromage factory.'

Chloe laughed and slapped his arm, 'aw c'mon Dan. I think he's kind of cute.'

Danny feigned indignation, 'cute, *cute*?' He rolled up one eyelid and turned to face her, 'the guy has a paunch Chloe my dear, and he has a hunched back,' he pulled up one shoulder and gurned at her, imitating the voice of Joseph Merrick, the elephant man, *'he looksh like shomething out of a freak show.'*

'That may be so Daniel, but,' she tucked her hair behind her ear and pouted her lips, 'he seems very good with his hands.'

Danny aped a face full of shock and indignation but smiled nonetheless, 'not as good as mine my darling.'

Chloe sniggered and pointed at her daughter, Laura, who was sitting near the front of the crowd and gasping at every magic trick and act of slapstick tomfoolery. 'She's loving it,' she picked up her phone and took a couple of photos of Laura smiling while the comedic Mister Trick danced across the stage like he was treading on hot coals, 'we'll have to book him for Laura's birthday party.'

'We'll see. Depends on how much he charges.'

Meanwhile Muriel's alcohol consumption was ramping up alongside her acidic cynicism and acrid bitterness, 'this bloke should be, *hic*, ashamed of himself. Look at the, *hic*, state of him,' she leaned over Ruth, who was nodding off after her significant buffet consumption and hollered loudly to George, the diminutive eighty-two year old chairman of the local grass bowls club. 'Tell me this George. Would you be seen, *hic*, dead going out looking like....' she swung our her arm and flailed in the direction of the stage, knocking an empty wine glass over in the process, '*that*?'

George pushed his spectacles up his nose, sipped on his half pint of dark and mild, wiped his mouth with the back of his hand and grunted. 'Well, probably not Muriel but now is a different time after all,' he brushed his long comb-over across the top of his thinning pate, 'there's a lot of things that kids do nowadays that I wouldn't be seen dead doing. Especially not all that twitchering and internetting.'

'Well itsh a bloody dishgrace, thatsh what, *hic*, it ish....'

Lydia glared over at her mother who she could see was going to be trouble later in the evening and swigged on her lemonade. At least one of them needed to remain sober, she thought. Somebody needed to be the responsible adult. She looked over at Drew who was still gaping in awe at Rufus in his bloody makeup and glad-rags and tutted. Well, she rused, if he was going to stand there all night playing at being the magician's beautiful assistant she was going to have a drink or three. She leaned over the bar.

'Debbie, can you get me a double vodka and coke, with ice. Thanks darling.'

Debbie Pratt, the pretty forty-something blond who, by all accounts, was having an affair with the social committee chairman, winked at her.

'Had enough of this already my love?'

'No, no. It's fine. He's getting on my nerves a bit but I can cope with that.'

Debbie handed her a tall, ice cold glass of dark-brown, carbonated liquid. The ice cubes clinked as Lydia picked it up and swirled it from side to side, mixing the vodka with the sugary cola. 'The kids seem to love him.'

'Well,' Lydia took a large sip and sighed as the alcohol warmly slid down her throat, 'that's good enough for me then.'

'Okay, okay, ladies and gentlemen boys and girls. Mister Trick,' the magician smiled, winked and pointed at his chest, 'that's me.' The kids laughed. 'Mister Trick is going to take a short break so that he can prepare for the big finale in the second act,' the boys and girls oohed. 'And also,' he crossed his legs and pursed his lips, 'I need to have a pee pee.' The children sniggered, 'but after the break you are going to see magic like you have never seen and that you will likely never see again.'

'Oh, *hic*, pull the other one.' Muriel was trying to stand up but Ruth, shaken from her slumber, leaned over and pulled her down by the sleeve of her blouse.

Mister Trick glared at her but gave her no mind. 'There will be BOOMS,' he punched the air, 'BANGS,' he clapped his hands, 'and a tremendous cacophony, the sight or sound of which should never be seen or heard at home,' he gazed down at the kids and whispered, his forefinger placed on his lips, 'especially when your parents are looking.' The kids laughed, a few looking back nervously at their mums and dads. Mister Trick looked across at Drew and nodded, 'so with that my friends I bid you adieu and I will back in less than two shakes of an elephant's bottom.'

He waved his hands in front of him as if swatting an errant fly. There was a pop, a large puff of dry ice and he was gone.

The kids all stood up, their faces a delicate cocktail of surprise and awe as they broke out in jubilant elation, roaring and clapping their hands loudly in approval.

Tabitha burst into tears at the site of the funny magician seemingly vanishing into thin air and Tara leaned over the pushchair to collect her into her arms. 'Now, now Tabitha dear. It's just a magic trick, that's all, that's all,' she tickled her tummy and kissed her cheek, 'come to Auntie, I'll take good care of you. I will always take good care of you' she looked across the hall at her sister, holding court as she always did, the men flocking around her like flies around...well. And her mother, knocking back the grape like there was no tomorrow and complaining about almost everything to very nearly everyone. And her brother, her mother's favourite, the apple of her eye, the rather hefty and ever so slightly aggressive pull on her not so long, yet fiercely retractable apron strings. 'I hope we don't have to hang around for too long,' she glanced over at Eli, 'I'm not sure I could take any more of it. Let's just get this over and done with.' He smiled at her and nodded. He agreed. Tara's family were an acquired taste and one that he was never likely to savour.

Chloe towed her partner, Danny, onto the dancefloor as the tinny stereo kicked back into gear and 'I'm in the Mood for Dancing' by the Nolan Sisters leapt timidly out of the speakers.

'I love this one Danny,' she cried as she spun round and around, a glass of wine in one hand and her reluctant dance partner's arm in the other, 'this is my *jaaaam*.'

Lydia, increasingly frustrated at the lack of attention from her husband and more than a little elated at her much younger and rather estranged sister taking the heavy load of looking after their daughter, eagerly followed suit.

'This reminds me of our school disco Chloe, do you remember?' she waved her arms in the air and whirled around, her long dress swirling round her like a whirligig.

'What a night that was Lyd'. You and that bloke from year thirteen,' Chloe put a hand to her chin, 'that was it, Raul, the Spanish exchange guy.'

Lydia threw her head back and laughed, 'oh yes. Raul,' she clapped and tapped her feet as if in the wild throes of a flamenco dance, 'Raul of the dark hair, dark complexion, soft hands and even softer lips.'

Danny slowly withdrew himself from the conversation and headed to the bar, winking at Eli as if to say, 'I got myself out of that one.' Eli's face remained passive as Tara gently rocked Tabitha in her arms.

Chloe leaned over and coyly whispered into Lydia's ear, 'your brother didn't take too much to Raul that night as I remember.'

'What do you mean?'

Chloe smiled as she glanced around her, 'well, if my memory serves me well, which it always does,' she danced around Lydia like a colourful and slightly inebriated whirling dervish, 'Shawn caught you two out in the bike sheds with his mediterranean hand up your way too-tight skirt.'

Lydia slapped her playfully on the bum, 'Chloe Harper! I can't believe you remember that!'

Chloe cooed at her in mock surprise, 'I remember a great many things Lydia my dear,' she peered at her through her drunken haze, 'a great many.'

Lydia paused as she remembered that night, 'but you're right,' her eyes glazed over as the three double vodkas and a tequila that she'd downed in quick succession started to cast a gentle fog over her senses, 'Shawn didn't like Raul. And he definitely didn't like....'

'Drew?' Chloe laughed, 'no he didn't like Drew. And neither did you. In fact you both hated him and his lunatic of a brother, Arthur,' she paused as the next song started to wheeze out of the bargain store stereo. 'Dancing Queen? You've gotta be kidding me.' She grabbed Lydia's hand and spun her around as Sandra and Shawn Darling glided onto the dancefloor. 'Shawn, I was just reminding Lyd' about how much you two hated Drew and Arthur Hermann at school.'

Shawn grunted, 'yep. Both a couple of hopeless losers as far as I was concerned.' Sandra glared at him and he paused. 'But Drew's the father of my niece now so he's family and that's all there is to it.'

Chloe pointed at Shawn and Lydia in turn, 'but you both *haaaated* them *soooo baaad*.' She glided between the three of them while gawping at them playfully in turn, 'I mean, it was verging on some kind of evil form of vindictiveness, like you were out to get them or something, like they'd done something to you. You called them...' she half tripped but caught herself and whirled around, 'you called them the Shit-stains,' she half chuckled, 'everyday it was like *hey, there's Shit-stain number 1 with his even uglier brother, Shit-stain number 2. Hey Shit-stains, how's your Shit-stained day? What do you call a Shit-stain's dad? Mr Shit-stain. Where do Shit-stains go on holiday? Shit-stainland.*'

Lydia put a finger to Chloe's pursed lips, 'shhhh you idiot,' she giggled, 'that's my husband now you know.'

Chloe halted on the spot and looked at her feet in faux shame, 'you're right Lyd'. She slowly raised her head, a grin spread across her face like strawberry jam on toast, 'that means you must be *Mrs Shit-stain.*' She guffawed so loud that spittle sprayed across Lydia's cheeks and she wiped it off in laughing disgust.

'You're disgraceful Chloe, you really are.'

Sandra Darling could see her husband was visibly shaking and she touched his arm tenderly. 'Girls, be a little more tactful please,' she ran a finger down her husband's neck, 'remember what happened.'

Muriel and Ruth leapt up onto the dancefloor as 'It's Not Unusual' by Tom Jones trickled out of the PA system. 'C'mon you lot, *hic*, now this is a real song by a,,*hic*, a real man. Ain't I right, *hic*, Ruthie?'

Ruth, her jowls vibrating as she gently swung her hips, smiled sheepishly, 'oh yes Muriel. He was my cup of tea alright, although not a patch on my Albert.'

Muriel, two stepping from side to side, a half filled glass of wine held precariously in her right hand, rolled her eyes in dismay, 'yeah, yeah that's right Ruthie. Your Albert was a, *hic*, veritable heartthrob, we know.'

'We were just saying about what Arthur Hermann did to your Shawnee, mother-in-law.' Sandra was still rubbing her husband's arm as the red veins in his temples pulsed and his mottled skin rippled.

Muriel hissed through her teeth, 'those boys were always trouble. Always,' she cursed as she spilled some wine onto the floor, 'what he did to my Shawnee was....unforgiveable,' she peered over her glasses at Barbara, 'I hope that Arthur rots in that mental home they locked him up in.'

Chloe, seemingly oblivious to the right angled tangent their conversation had taken and even more unaware of the intensifying rage burning inside Shawn Darling, interjected. 'Wait a minute, weren't you two involved when Arthur lost an eye?'

Sandra gulped and Muriel choked on her sauvignon blanc. Lydia glared at Chloe through bloodshot, mascara streaked eyes. Shawn's face darkened to a deeper shade of purple.

'Now, now Chloe,' Lydia put an arm around Chloe's shoulders as they both swayed to the music, 'that was never proven. Sure there were rumours but no-one ever solved the mystery of who hurled that rock at Drew and his brother. I mean,' she mustered a half-hearted chuckle, 'it's absurd. Why would Shawn and I be involved in such a thing, really?'

'But you were there,' Chloe peered at Lydia and then up at Shawn, 'right?'

Shawn Darling brushed his wife's caress away and leaned in towards Chloe who took a half step backwards, nudging into Danny who was athletically sliding across the dancefloor to bring her a jack and coke. 'Listen to your friend Chloe. We weren't there and no-one ever found out who did it,' his veins were bulging under his scarred skin, the pink and purple texture rippling and twitching, 'all they managed to find out was that Drew and Arthur were somewhere where they had no place in being at a time they shouldn't have been and they obviously ran into some trouble that they weren't well equipped to handle.' Shawn rubbed a hand across his scar vigorously as if it was itching furiously, 'all I know is that when Arthur returned to school he was hell-bent on some misguided notion of revenge. He grabbed a lit Bunsen burner in chemistry class, attacked me with it, whilst unprovoked I might add, and torched the skin from my neck and shoulder, setting my hair and school blazer alight and almost killing me in the process.' He reached out and placed a huge, shaking hand on her shoulder, 'if anyone should be angry about what happened that school year it's me, so if you've got something to say Chloe, I suggest you say it now.'

Danny took hold of a startled and somewhat frightened Chloe's arm and pulled her protectively behind him. He took a step towards Shawn, the top of his head barely reaching the tip of Shawn's nose, and sneered defiantly at him, 'I suggest you leave my girlfriend alone scarface or we'll have to take this outside.'

Muriel and Ruthie took two steps back, half anticipating the dancefloor tussle, Lydia swayed from side to side, one eye closed to steady her focus and Sandra attempted to grab Shawn's huge forearm.

'We don't need to do that Danny, you jumped up little weasel,' Shawn rolled up his shirt cuffs, 'we can do it *riiiiight* here.....'

With a flash, a boom and puff of smoke Mister Truck did a dramatic forward roll across the dance floor and then a slightly clumsy backward roll onto the stage.

'Ta Taaaaaaaaaaa!'

The children who were still on the dancefloor, leaping around the hall like hungry gibbons on energy drink highs, stopped dead in their tracks and the few that were still clinging to their parents sides, some of them feeling the effects of the late night shenanigans and the sugary come down from the sweets and ice cream, ran to the front of the stage.

'Come now children, come down to the front, *come on*. We have a stupendous magical mystery event to show you and it will blow your tiny little minds.'

The children all scooched up so that they were as close to Mister Trick as humanly possible without physically standing around him on the stage.

'This really is the big reveal kids, an event of such enormity, such gravitas, such stupendous significance and importance that I'm afraid,' he peered down and beamed a lipstick covered smile at them, 'that we need an adult volunteer.'

The kids groaned in disapproval.

'But don't worry one and all, we also need a child volunteer.' The children cheered in delight as Mister

Trick glared over at Tara, 'a very,' he glanced at the baby girl in her arms, 'young child'.

Drew pressed play on the CD player and a fanfare leapt from its boom box speaker system.

'You sire with the long hair and serious, yet histrionic face,' he pointed at Eli who was standing next to Tara at the side of the hall, 'will you please make your way to the front of the stage.'

The beleaguered Eli shook his head apologetically but, egged on by Lydia who was dragging him by his left arm, reluctantly stepped over the children with his long gangly legs and up onto the platform. He stood sheepishly to the magician's right hand side.

Mister Trick clapped him on the back and then turned to Tara.

'The lady with the pretty and the even more beee-eautiful baby. Will you please make your way to the front of the stage.'

Tara laughed, tickled Tabitha under the chin and stepped up onto the stage, this time to the magician's left hand side. She held Tabitha close and smiled eagerly at the crowd. She winked knowingly at Lydia.

'*Aaand* who do we have here,' he turned to Eli who was peering down at him from his elevated height, tipped his hat to one side as he did so, and asked 'what is your name dear sire.'

Eli responded in a hoarse and slightly muffled tone, 'my name is Eli.'

'Eli is it? Eli like the biblical character. You read the bible kids?' The children mumbled and murmured, 'nah. Me neither. It's too long, doesn't have enough pictures and the ending is way too depressing.'

Muriel muttered a, 'oh, really?'

'And you madam?' he turned to face Tara and Tabitha who was gurgling and talking in baby language, 'can I ask your name and the name of your baby?'

'Oh,' Tara blushed, 'she's not my baby......no, not really. I......my name is Tara and this is my niece, Tabitha.'

The amassed crowd cheered at the mention of the freshly christened Tabitha's name.

'Tabitha, what a beautiful name. I mean, not that Tara isn't a lovely name but Tabitha.....' he put his hands to his face, 'it just rolls off the tongue like a delightful sonnet or a lilting melody.'

He brushed a finger through Tabitha's curly hair and sighed.

'And who, may I ask, is the mother?'

Tara, pointed across the hall towards the glaringly intoxicated Lydia, 'my sister, over there, with the short, dark hair,' she smirked, 'Lydia Hermann.'

Mister Trick glanced at Drew and shrugged his shoulders. Drew sighed and looked around the hall; at Shawn who's face and neck were slowly fading from a deep purple to a reddish hue, at Lydia who was swaying from side to side with her right arm around Chloe's shoulders and at Muriel who was rolling her eyes and glugging on what was left of her wine. The famous Darling trio. He looked back at the magician and nodded.

'Can I ask that the children part in the middle like the red sea and let young Lydia Hermann through.'

Lydia jumped as if startled, turned to Chloe and mouthed a 'who me?'

Chloe smiled and mouthed back a 'yes, you!'

'Yes, you madam. As quick as you can, although you are paying me by the hour so, on second thoughts, take your time.' He faked a chuckle and pulled a long chain of colourful hankies out of one sleeve, much to the children's collective delight.

Lydia stumbled and staggered down the walkway between the young boys and girls, all of whom who were sitting with their mouths agape, wondering what the enigmatic and eccentric magician had in store for her.

Mister Trick reached out a hand and said 'STOP!'

Lydia stopped dead in her tracks and looked around her at her assorted friends and family. They were all staring at her like she was a mildly interesting exhibit at an old curiosity shop. She stood exposed and unsure of herself, like a child lost in a forbidden forest. She was around six feet from the front of the stage, Mister Trick in front of her, Eli to her left and Tara, cradling Tabitha in her arms, to her right. They looked down at her like the judge had at her hearing. She shuddered at the unwanted memory.

'That's far enough Lydia my dear,' he turned to face the enthralled Drew, 'Andrew my good sire. Would you do the honours?'

Drew Hermann shot a big smile at his wife, took a folding table from Mister Trick's trolley of trinkets and placed it next to Lydia, kissing her on the cheek as he did so. 'This is going to be so much fun. I can't wait.'

Lydia glared back at him through bloodshot eyes and frowned. 'What are you up to Drew?

'Don't worry Lyd'. All will be revealed,' he playfully pinched her cheek, 'you're gonna bloody love it.'

He then strode over to the rickety buffet table, placed a hand either side of the large, frosted christening cake, *'Our baby Tabitha'* emblazoned on the top in bold, pink icing, and carried it over to Lydia. He placed it gently onto the folding table now standing directly between Lydia and the animated Mister Trick.

'Thank you Andrew, thank you very much. Now children!' The children, all of whom had been waiting patiently as Mister Trick directed the adults around them like a conductor at a classical music revue, shuffled on the floor expectantly. 'I am going to do a trick so fantastic, so outrageous, so downright ridiculous that you will be talking about it at school for years, you will be reciting it to your workmates when you are approaching middle age and you will recount it to the nurse when you are old and have had too many sherries at the nursing home's Christmas party.'

'Oh come off it Mister, *hic*, no trick. Just get on with it.' Muriel glared over the top of her glasses and wiped wine from the corner of her mouth with the back of her withering hand. 'Are you going to do this trick or are we gonna have to stand around all night watching you prance around in those dodgy clothes and that, *hic*, girly make up.'

Mister Trick pulled up his trousers, tucked in his shirt, rubbed his nose and glanced nervously at Drew who was standing just off stage to his left. Drew nodded encouragingly. The magician could feel the nervous energy in his heart, the tingling in his fingers and his face felt hot and flushed. He had played the game to a fault so far but the old lady was beginning to get to him and he didn't know if he wanted to do the thing that Drew and....

'Wait a minute,' Shawn Darling looked around him and snarled, a look of profound realisation on his crimson face. He turned from the bemused and dumbfounded Lydia to the eagerly anticipating Drew and up at the increasingly disturbed and unsettled children's entertainer. He gesticulated aggressively at Mister Trick and announced, 'I know who he is ma'. He pulled free from his wife Sandra's grasp and took a giant step toward the stage, 'I know exactly who this joker is, and he's not going to get one over on us.'

Lydia looked back at her brother and frowned. Muriel set down her glass and walked to his side.

'What do you mean my Shawnee?'

Mister Trick, nee Rufus Trowbridge, glanced at Drew, lifted his hat, ran a hand through his sweaty hair, placed his hat back atop his head and laughed nervously.

'I don't know what you are insinuating dear sire, but if you would like to join in on the act you are,' he gulped, 'of course, most welcome.'

'*He* knows,' Shawn pointed at Drew, his face drawn down in a contorted sneer, 'he knows exactly who he is. I'd heard rumours that he'd got out, but I thought that was all they were,' he looked imploringly at his mother, 'you know? Just rumours.' He took another step towards the stage and rolled up his shirt sleeves, 'you....you step away from my sister, *Arthur Hermann*!'

Mister Trick grabbed his heart as if he had been shot, and pulled out a long colourful hanky from his breast pocket. He gingerly reached out to hand it to the enraged Shawn Darling, 'not me I'm afraid dear Shawn. But here, wipe your brow,' he looked at the children and winked, but he was fooling no-one, 'you look a little bit flustered.'

Before the children could laugh Shawn Darling grabbed Mister Trick's hand and yanked him towards him so hard that his hat flew from his head and landed on the stage between Eli and Tara. Starburst, humbugs, Licourice Allsorts, lemon sherberts and the like tumbled from the hat as it hit the floor, rolling haphazardly across the stage and resting askew like a hopeless drunk at midnight leaning against a moonlit lamp post.

Shawn grabbed Mister Trick by the mustard colour collar and shook him, 'if you've come back for some sort of revenge Arthur then let's have it out here and now,' he rubbed a large, calloused hand down his neck, 'I have some revenge of my own that I want to dish out,' he roared, 'and it's been a *bloody* long time coming!'

The children scattered left and right as Mister Trick shook himself from the iron grasp of his captor, bumped into a bemused Lydia and circled around the christening cake. Tara hugged Tabitha close to her breast and Drew watched nervously as his brother-in-law lunged at the magician over the top of the cake. Behind them Chloe grabbed her daughter Laura in her arms and they both circled behind Danny for protection. Together they slowly edged backwards towards the exit at the rear of the hall. 'Let's get out of here Danny. I've seen what happens when the Darling's get into one and it's not something that I want my Laura to witness.'

Mister Trick was dancing side to side like a shadow boxer behind the cake and narrowly keeping out of his pursuer's long and treacherous grasp, 'I don't know who you think I am dear sire, but I can assure you I am not this Arthur of which you speak.'

The assorted guests started to dissipate to the corners of the room as the scuffle unfolded, many of them grabbing their children and dragging them to the farthest point away from the ensuing violence. The remaining children stood up and ran, many of them crying.

'I can see it's you, you little twerp. A little older, a lot rounder, more jowly than I remember,' he swiped over the cake and narrowly missed Mister Trick's bulbous nose, 'but I know a glass eye when I see one.'

Lydia leered over the cake and looked at the magician, 'you know what Shawn,' she smiled, 'I think you're right. That's fucking Arthur Hermann alright, the little *shit-stain* that set you on fire,' she laughed hysterically, 'hey shit-stain. How was the shit-stained crazy hospital? Full of shit-stained loonies?' She shot a glance at Drew who was slowly backing away towards the exit. 'And *youuuu*. You bastard. You never told me that they'd let your lunatic brother out,' she pointed a shaking finger at him and spat, 'and you brought him here? You're bloody in on it!' she was enraged, her face twisted and snarling. 'After you convinced me you'd changed, that you'd become normal. After I'd let you into my family. *How dare you!*'

Muriel raced to her son's side, 'well I'll be a monkey's aunt. I think you're right kids. That's the little sod that tried to kill my Shawnee. These Hermann's can't be trusted Lydia. I always told, *hic*, you that!'

Shawn Darling reached over the cake, grabbed the magician by his throat, reached out his other hand and stuck his large, gnarly forefinger and his hooked, wart covered thumb into Mister Trick's left eye. He pinched hard and pulled. The magician gave out a piercing shriek like a cat in distress and a couple of the adults and a few of the kids retched and gagged.

'What the hell....' Shawn pulled his hand away and looked disbelievingly at the flimsy object he had clasped between his thumb and finger. It hung like a piece of flaccid loose skin with a discombobulated iris that was slightly off centre. 'A contact lens?' Shawn looked at the flat, miniature eye like it was the strangest, most odd thing he had ever seen. 'Who the hell *are* you?'

Mister Trick ran a hand through his slick hair, pulled up his trousers, brushed down his shirt, stood back from the cake and smiled. When he spoke his voice was an octave deeper and a touch less regal. 'Rufus Trowbridge, Shawn.' he took off his purple waistcoat and passed it to Drew, his stomach sagging over his belt, his slightly hairy belly button exposed. 'I...er...clean the windows at your brother-in-law's shop,' he scratched his ear and smirked, 'I thought you knew that,' he held out his hands apologetically, 'I...I only did it for the money,' he blinked and frowned, 'although they only paid me a ton fifty. Probably not worth it really. I turned down another, better paid gig at the town hall to come here and dress up like this,' he pulled at his dress shirt, 'to entertain these kids and be a part of this...ruse. They...' he pointed at Drew and Eli, 'they wanted a distraction, like a card trick, you know? I show you my right hand with the full deck in it and with my left hand I pull out the extra card that you don't see. The one that matches the card that I've given you and that you think you've hidden away in amongst all the other cards. It was just,' he wiped his sweaty and slick hair out of his eyes, 'it was just a bit of fun really. They said it was going to be a big surprise, you know? The reunion and all that.' Rufus smiled gingerly, looked up at Drew, across at Eli and back at Shawn. 'Although I can see it's not a happy reunion. No, not happy at all,' he wiped the sweat from his top lip with the back of his shirt sleeve, 'and not one that I want to continue being a part of. I think I'll just call time and bid my adieu.' And with that he lifted his arm, waved a nervous, unsteady hand and swiftly exited through the double doors.

'But the eye.....the hat....' Shawn looked at his sister Lydia and his mother Muriel, both of whom stood beside him around the large, white cake atop the folding table, and then looked back at his wife Sandra who appeared befuddled and more than a little ashamed. Then he looked up at the stage.

The hat and the waistcoat were gone.

Suddenly there was a noise like a marble hitting wood, and a rolling sound like a bowling ball travelling slowly down the alley of a ten pin bowling rink. Lydia, Muriel and Shawn looked down at the glass eyeball as it rolled to a stop by Lydia's bare, size five feet. She bent down and picked it up.

Her brow furrowed in confusion and barely stifled trepidation. 'What?'

'I think you'll find that's mine....*sister-in-law*.'

The three of them looked up at the stage; at Lydia and Shawn's younger sister, Tara, the sister that had never really felt part of the Darling family, the trio with the elusive familial bond that had been forged by the terrible acts of her siblings; at Tabitha who was cuddling into her auntie and absent mindedly twisting her tiny finger playfully around Tara's long, blond hair; at Drew who had stepped up onto the stage and was wrapping his arms protectively around Tara and Tabitha, a look of sad disapproval on his sombre face and at Eli, the tall silent brother-in-law with the long hair, long face, the tall, slender frame, the hat with the colourful sweets attached to it in a velvety, sugary unison, the purple, crushed velvet waistcoat and the black and lonely void of an empty eye socket. Eli wiped his hand down his cheek, removing the skin coloured make up that he had painted there earlier that day and a blue, tear shaped tattoo appeared.

The throng of guests gasped.

Shawn turned to him.

'*You….*'

Eli, nee Arthur Hermann, *nee Mister Trick*, smiled and withdrew a light brown, spindly stick from the inside pocket of his jacket, pointed it at the cake, closed his eyes and mouthed a silent incantation.

The large white cake began to turn as piercing carousel music played from invisible speakers, its soulless melody filling the room like a noxious gas.

Muriel pushed her glasses up her vein-ridden nose and stared at the whirling cake. Lydia grabbed a hold of her brother's bulging arm in the overly affectionate way that had always agitated Shawn's wife and watched as the pink lettering whirled around and around in a hypnotic dance. Shawn gasped as a twelve centimetre hole appeared in the top of the cake and a metallic tube started to appear. As the cake span and the music played and the guests grew afraid for their lives and started to evacuate the hall, hastily herding their children out through the exit doors like little lambs, the Darling trio became more and more entranced by the whirling, iced delicacy in front of them. They leaned in closely as one to look. The metallic tube emerged from the cake like a glorious erection, followed by a round, polished base, attached to which was a red coloured valve and a long plastic pipe. Muriel looked at Lydia and Lydia looked at Shawn and they all said in unison;

'A Bunsen burner!'

The burner, its gleaming, sleek features glistening with the reflection of the LED gloriousness of the spinning disco lights, tilted to its side, gave out a hiss and a shriek and, while Shawn, Muriel and Lydia turned to flee, it emitted a flame so ferocious and vast that it engulfed the hapless trio in its voluptuous and tempestuous energy. Before anyone could say 'Mister Trick' they were ablaze and staggering around the cake like angrily animated roman candles on Guy Fawkes night.

Shawn Darling's already mottled neck caught first, the tender skin splitting and flapping, the fat underneath bubbling like bacon rind and his muscle tendons snapping from his heavy bones like rubber bands. Lydia's hair erupted like the tip of a match, flames erupted from her eyes and mouth as she screamed a furious oath of vengeance and her bare feet shrivelled as the flesh peeled away like overly cooked barbecue pulled pork. Muriel's spectacles melted instantly to her face as her eyeballs popped, her dentures disintegrated onto her boiling tongue and the loose skin hanging from her arms shrivelled and blackened. Within seconds their whirling and thrashing forms were completely engulfed.

Fu fu (Andrew Hermann's childhood name for his ever so slightly older twin brother, Arthur) stood with his arm outstretched, waving his Poplar wand from right to left while dressed in the colourful top hat and waistcoat of he and his brother's imaginary childhood magician friend Mister Trick, the friend that would carry out various acts of devilry and mischief in their name, including the day long incarceration of their cousin Douglas in the school broom cupboard and the kidnap and ultimate murder of their next door neighbour, Mrs. Attwood's, beloved cat Ginger. Ro Dro (Arthur Hermann's childhood name for his ever so slightly younger twin brother, Andrew) laughed with un-supressed joy and delight and Tara, Tabitha in her arms and purring at the pretty colours flailing around the dance floor, smiled with a sense of sweet satisfaction. How Tara loved her beloved Arthur and how she hated her mother (so full of bile and venom), her brother (so angry and consumed with desire for vengeance and wrath) and sister (so obsessed with her own brother and so wasteful of the blessed life and beautiful daughter she had with the dutiful Andrew).

As the hall vacated and the fire alarm blasted all around them Arthur reached down, retrieved his perfectly spherical eye from the burning wreckage of the Darling trio, blew on it's warm surface to cool it and placed it firmly back in its vacant socket. He straightened his waistcoat, tilted his hat to one side, kissed his wife, his brother and his niece and smiled with a deep sense of retribution. Together they stepped down from the stage, arm in arm and cheek to cheek and left through the double doors, their transit van parked just outside and awaiting the return of the glorious victors.

Ruthie sat at the back of the empty hall in the shadows, her brown wig slanted to the side of her rotund face, her skin bubbling and flexing as she gradually returned to her original form. She watched in grim comfort as the scorching flames diminished into glowing, fatty embers, the bones and ashes of the estranged wife and children of Petroc Darling scattered across the blackened floor like empty seed husks. She smiled, exposing her blackened teeth, as the three co-plotters and their baby departed, the chaos that they had caused planted firmly in their rear view mirrors. She smiled when she thought of Arthur and Andrew Hermann, the descendants of the child that she had spawned with Alexander Hermann, nee Hermann the Great, the famous French conjurer who she had taken as a lover in the late eighteen hundreds. She laughed knowingly at how disturbed and removed from reality they had become. Just like their great, great, great grandfather, she thought. She glared at the disgustingly soft and gentle Darling child, Tabitha, and the remaining daughter of the treacherous Petroc, Tara. There was time for them later, she mused. Right know they had served a purpose. After all, Morai did not need to fret with the passing of time. Time was her friend and she of it. Her vengeance was unending and unyielding. Her compassion was pure but fleeting. She placed her black, crooked hat atop her head, pulled her long, slate grey cape around her slender body and smiled in exaltation. It was time that she returned to Fey.

ABOUT THE AUTHOR

Stacey Dighton is a married father of two from Kent, England. He and his wife, Jo, enjoy hiking with their Bassett Hound, Lily, and spending time with their adult children, Jayden and Harley. The family are keen music lovers and enjoy attending gigs and festivals whenever they can.

Printed in Great Britain
by Amazon

43200144R00158